DEATH
IN
STORE

DEATH
IN
STORE

Jennifer Rowe

A Perfect Crime Book

DOUBLEDAY

NEW YORK   LONDON   TORONTO   SYDNEY   AUCKLAND

A PERFECT CRIME BOOK

Published by Doubleday
a division of Bantam Doubleday Dell Publishing Group, Inc.
666 Fifth Avenue, New York, New York 10103

DOUBLEDAY is a trademark of Doubleday, a division
of Bantam Doubleday Dell Publishing Group, Inc.

Book design by Tasha Hall

Library of Congress Cataloging-in-Publication Data

Rowe, Jennifer.
Death in store / by Jennifer Rowe.
p.   cm.
"A Perfect crime book."
I. Title.
PR9619.3.R6276D4   1993
823—dc20   92-28217
CIP

ISBN 0-385-42598-8
Copyright © 1993 by Jennifer Rowe
All Rights Reserved
Printed in the United States of America
January 1993
First Edition in the United States of America

DEATH
IN
STORE

FORBIDDEN
FRUIT

DETECTIVE SERGEANT DAN TOBY considered the ghost of Christmas past. Not Christmas Day, eating hot turkey and tinned pudding and custard at his in-laws' place in the sweltering heat, wearing a wilting paper hat that leaked colour onto his sweating forehead. No, not that. But Christmas Eve, coming home in the relative cool of the evening, to David, always eight or nine in this kind of memory, and to Evelyn, pretty and welcoming and not yet sick of his work, and the worry, and the hours he kept, and, finally, him. And the house bright with decorations and smelling of pine needles and fruit cake. And a sense of excitement, David crackling with it, and Christmas specials on TV, and last-minute presents to be wrapped.

Toby pushed his chair back from his battered desk, looked around the almost deserted department and considered Christmas Eve present. It didn't take long. There was nothing to it. No wife, no child, no Christmas tree—and no in-laws' Christmas lunch to look forward to, if it came to that. Well, every cloud had a silver

3

lining. Of course he'd get a call from David tomorrow morning, early, from wherever he was—Frankfurt, wasn't it? And later he'd drive up to the mountains, like most years, to his brother Simon. Spend a few days contemplating the scenery, having a break. He'd probably enjoy it, once he got there. Last year he'd been on duty over Christmas. Everyone had commiserated with him, and he'd grumbled dutifully about it. But in his heart, he realised, he'd been glad. This year he'd have to get through the festive season unpropped by work, or routine, and meet his ghosts head on. Not a compelling prospect.

He began unwillingly to poke the papers on his desk into some sort of order. He'd been off duty for an hour. No point in hanging around, using the place as some sort of security blanket. People would start noticing, start feeling sorry for him. The thought made him stand up quickly, tap pockets for keys and wallet, turn off the desk lamp. Now he couldn't get out of the place fast enough.

He shouted a few vague greetings to the unwilling on-duty staff and headed down the corridor to the lifts.

"Have a good one, Dan," one of the policewomen called after him. "Merry Christmas!"

Merry Christmas.

Someone had stuck plastic mistletoe over the lift button. A nice thought, but you'd have to be a dwarf to take advantage of it. He stabbed at the button gloomily, and at almost the same moment the lift doors opened. He stepped inside, still sunk in thought, and almost collided with a small, wiry person sauntering out.

"For God's sake!" Toby looked down at her. "Birdie, what're you doing here?"

"Looking for you," she replied off-handedly.

They bolted into the lift together as the doors began to slide shut. Nonplussed, Toby stared at his companion.

"I thought I'd see if you'd like a drink," Verity Birdwood shrugged. "Thought you might be feeling like company. Seeing as it's Christmas Eve."

"At a loose end, are you?" snapped Toby. He was horrified to find just how pleased he was to see her.

She shrugged again, her eyes behind the thick glasses fixed on the door.

Toby thought of driving off alone to his dark, hot house, picking up some takeaway food on the way, watching TV alone with his ghosts. He thought of the ribbing he'd get from his colleagues if anyone saw him hobnobbing off duty with this odd little person who set herself up, they all knew, as some sort of amateur detective. He considered the possibility that she was up to something, wanting information, for example, or a look at some file she wasn't supposed to even know existed, or something else that would lead him into trouble and strife. Then he thought of sitting for an hour or two opposite those intelligent amber eyes, being irritated and amused, having a few drinks and some food in company, noise and light.

He grinned broadly. "Why not? God only knows, I've got nothing better to do."

Birdie said nothing. The lift doors opened and she edged past him and wandered off down the corridor towards the exit. Toby followed slowly, his hands in his pockets. By the time he joined her at the big front doors, he was onto his second chorus of "Good King Wenceslas."

"What I'd like to know, I really would, is why you're so interested in all this, Birdwood?" Toby was feeling expansive and comfortable. The pub was air-conditioned, the food had been good, someone was playing the piano, and Birdie was being less irritating than usual, as if mellowed, at least temporarily, by the night, or the season. She had listened intelligently to several reminiscences of his past cases, asked some good leading questions, and generally acted like she really liked listening to him talk for a change, instead of holding forth herself.

"You mean, by 'all this,' murder cases, I presume?" asked Birdie coolly. "Why shouldn't I be? *You* are."

"Yes, but I'm a bloody policeman, aren't I?" he argued. "It's my job to be interested. For you it's like a sort of hobby. Pretty funny hobby."

"It's just problem-solving, Dan," said the small woman reasonably. "If I went in for brainteasers or chess you wouldn't think it was funny."

"Well, it wouldn't be, would it?" Toby shook his head, feeling a little muzzled after the last beer. He tried again. "People die in murder cases. It's not just a game, where the answer doesn't matter to anyone but the person playing. It's real."

She spread out her hands. "Exactly," she said, and finished her drink.

He stared at her in silence for a minute. Her glasses gleamed in the light. "I'll get some more," she said, and went over to the bar.

"How did it start then?" he asked, when she had returned with two more beers. He looked ruefully at his frothing glass. It looked good, but at this rate he'd have to get a cab home. If he could find one. "Did you read those books, those thrillers, when you were young, or what?"

She nodded. "Oh, yes, I read Agatha Christie and all that. I liked them. But I don't think I'd read many by the time I saw my first murder. Of course I was only a kid."

"What?"

She nodded. "Only fourteen. And I only discovered detective stories in second-year high school, so I hadn't really had time . . ."

He leaned back in his chair and grinned at her. "You're putting me on."

"No, I'm not!" she said indignantly. "It's absolutely true. I was fourteen and a bit. It was the man next door. And in fact, I was the one who really solved the murder, in the end."

"Oh, I'm sure." Toby sipped at his beer and felt good. Birdie was on form tonight all right.

Birdie leaned belligerently over the tabletop and scowled at him. "I promise you, Dan, it's absolutely true. Do you want to hear?"

"Why not? It's Christmas Eve. Perfect night for a fairytale." Toby leaned his head on his hand. "Go on, then. Once upon a time . . ."

"Every Christmas Eve, when I was a kid," Birdie began determinedly, "there'd be a party in one of the houses in our street. They took it in turns to play host, you see, but the same people would be there every year, and everyone would bring some food and something to drink, so the host wouldn't have to go to too much trouble."

"That's a good, old-fashioned idea," Toby interrupted approvingly. "You don't hear of that sort of thing much nowadays."

"A good thing too, in my view," muttered Birdie. "As you'll see if you can keep quiet for more than thirty seconds at a time."

"Oh, beg your pardon, pray proceed. I won't say another word."

"Okay. Well, most of the people were fairly well-off, and most of them didn't have kids. In fact, I was the only one in the street during the period these parties were going on. I never wanted to go to the party. I was glad to be left at home with the housekeeper, who'd play games with me and let me stay up and eat lollies and all that, and when I was older, watch TV with me till it closed, and it was Christmas Day." She shot a look at Toby, as if daring him to comment on the innocent enjoyments of her past, but he simply smiled at her blandly, and she continued.

"This particular Christmas Eve, though, it was different. My . . . my mother had died, during that year. My father didn't want to go out and leave me—or, I suppose now, go to the party alone. But all the neighbours were putting the pressure on for him to go. It'd been such a tradition, and I guess they thought it'd cheer him up. So he asked me if I'd go with him and of course I said I would, dreading it, because I wasn't much of a socialiser, to put it mildly, even in those days. And I knew I wasn't exactly a Pears advertisement, if you know what I mean—smiley, and pretty, like all these people expected young girls to be.

"But underneath all the dread was a sort of sneaking fascination. I'd been hearing about these parties for years. Now I was going to see one. They were a bit competitive about the decorations, apparently, and tried to outdo each other every year doing a beautiful tree and all that stuff, so that was one thing. And the food, of course, was an issue, because everyone brought their own special Christmas treat. But mainly it was because I was old enough by then to have heard the gossip about Sweet William and Peaches Macguire, and so—"

"Hold on!" Toby threw up an unbelieving hand. "What were those names again?"

"Peaches Macguire," said Birdie coldly, "and Sweet William. Peaches was the woman who lived next door to us in a huge house that looked like a castle. Actually castellated, it was. She was one of those incredibly fair, baby-soft women with that very opaque, perfect, pink and white skin. She was very pretty and giggly and sentimental, and she was married to this big businessman, quite a bit older than she was, called Jonathon Macguire. He was a huge, bull-necked, red-faced bloke—and very tough, or so my father always said. But he was very soft on Peaches. Adored her, and showered her with absolutely everything she wanted. And he was very jealous. I remember Mum talking about that, and saying how pathetic it was, and that he should have more sense. But Dad said it was no wonder, with Peaches so pretty and flirting with every man in sight, and then running back and cuddling up to Jonathon like a kitten. He reckoned the poor bugger never knew what to think, from one minute to the next.

"But Peaches and Jonathon seemed to get on all right, until one day old Mrs. Beady opposite died and William Tilbury moved into her little house. Mrs. Beady's house was just like a gingerbread cottage—you know the sort of thing—which was very appropriate for William, who was in fact a pastrycook. He had his own shop. Sweet William, it was called, so everyone called him that, too.

"Sweet William was young, and dark, and very good looking. And he was gentle and sensitive and sweet, with eyes like melting chocolate, and long, black lashes. The women all thought he was wonderful. The shop did a roaring trade because William was a wonderful cook, and half his customers were half in love with him and never missed a chance to pop in for a dozen Danish or a cake.

"But from the beginning, it seemed, Sweet William only had eyes for one woman—Peaches Macguire. He was nice to everyone in the street, friendly and charming and very obliging. But when Peaches was around he'd go quiet, and just watch her with big, swimming brown eyes as though he was under some sort of spell."

Toby was unable to contain himself. "Birdwood, are you having a lend of me or something? I've never heard such drivel in my life! I don't believe a word of it."

She shrugged. "Okay, if you don't like it I'll stop. You asked. Doesn't matter to me." She bent over her drink and sipped unconcernedly.

There was a short silence. The piano player started experimenting with "As Time Goes By." Toby cleared his throat. "The little swine got into her pants eventually, I suppose?" he asked casually.

Birdie raised her eyebrows. "I thought you weren't interested?"

"I didn't say that. I just said . . . Anyway, you've gone this far, go on. Go on, you know you're dying to. Stop sulking. We may as well have the whole catastrophe."

"As it happens," Birdie went on cheerily, "catastrophe is the perfect word for it. Sweet William's thing about Peaches Macguire became a huge item in our street. The thing was, you see, that it didn't wear off. It just got more and more obvious. By the time the Christmas Eve party I'm talking about happened, Peaches had been adored by William for over three years, and everyone could see that it was starting to wear her down. It was as though she'd tried all the little spells she knew to ward him off—being sweet and friendly in that hands-off way, talking about her husband a lot, all that. But nothing worked. William kept on adoring, and languishing, and looking tormented. And Jonathon got angrier and angrier and harder and harder with it. And the angrier and harder he got with Peaches, the softer and sweeter Sweet William must have looked to her. Romantic adoration's a pretty hard thing to resist, for some women. So I've heard.

"By November, people were saying a blow-up was inevitable before Christmas. They were just about evenly divided. The cynics said Peaches knew what side her bread was buttered on, and would very soon tell William straight to get out of their lives so that she and her rich and lawful husband could live happily ever after in their castle. The romantics preferred the view that she'd become quite as besotted with Sweet William as he was with her, and that they'd very soon run off together and live happily ever after in a rose-coloured cloud. They were both wrong, as it happened. But they were right about the timing.

"That year the Christmas Eve party was at the Macguires'

place. Under the circumstances it wasn't the ideal venue, but it was their turn, and Jonathon and Peaches didn't say anything, and no one else liked to suggest a change. So everyone turned up as usual, with the special food they always brought, and hoped for the best. My mother had always made shortbread for the party, so Dad went to Sweet William's and bought some for us to take.

"The Macguires had gone to just as much trouble as usual. There was a beautiful tree, standing in a corner by the food table, covered in tiny red and green fairy lights, and little silver baubles, hundreds of them. There were Christmas bells and real English holly in the fireplace, dim lights, and candles and Christmas carols playing. Peaches was smiling, but seemed a bit breathless and spaced-out. She was clinging to Jonathon's arm, looking very soft and fair in a gold-coloured dress. He wasn't taking much notice of her, or saying much, just serving drinks and welcoming people in his usual confident way. But he was standing up straighter than usual, I thought. He really looked quite impressive that night.

"So we put our shortbread on the table with Peaches' pâtés and terrines and Joan Brin's mince pies and all the other things, and got ourselves a drink to hold, and, along with everyone else, watched the door. Waiting for Sweet William.

"He came in last, carrying a big white box, looking straight-away for Peaches. When he saw her with Jonathon he smiled, just for a moment, very gently at her, then turned away and began to unpack his offering on the food table.

"It was a white sugar tree. I thought it was plastic at first, but William told me it was all made of sugar, and while he was un-packing it he told me how it was made. He was always very nice to me, as he was to everyone, in an absentminded sort of way. My mother had told me Sweet William always brought a Christmas tree dessert, but I hadn't imagined anything like this.

"William put the tree on the table, next to the real Christmas

11

tree, so that the fairy lights and silver balls made glows and shadows on the glittering sugar. Then he started to hang marzipan fruit on the branches, talking to me all the time. I suppose it was a relief to have a child to talk to. You could have cut the atmosphere in that room with a knife. The fruit was from his shop, he said, but he made the tree especially for this party every year. There was one piece of fruit for everyone, every piece was different, and he hadn't forgotten me, he said. He was quite a kind man, really. He talked and talked, and hung up these beautiful miniature fruits on his beautiful miniature tree as if nothing was wrong at all. But his fingers were trembling, and he was breathing hard, as if he'd been running. I pretended not to notice.

"William took quite a long time arranging his fruit, and getting the tree at just the right angle on the table and everything, and in the meantime the party seemed to get back underway. People started talking and laughing—I suppose they'd all had a few drinks by then and, after all, nothing awful had happened when William walked through the door, so they just got on with having fun like always. I went and stood beside Dad, and tried to merge into the curtains so no one would try to talk to me. All anyone could ever think of to say was 'How's school?' anyway, and since I was now on holidays, even that was pretty much a nonstarter.

"I looked around and saw Jonathon Macguire at the food table. He started to help himself to some pâté and stuff. Peaches wasn't with him anymore. He stuffed the food in his mouth and stood looking at William's tree, chewing. It glittered there, white, pink and green under the fairy lights, like something alive and magic, and the little fruits on its branches looked incredibly real. Jonathon put out his hand and touched one of the branches with a thick, blunt finger. A little piece of sugar fell onto the tablecloth, and he frowned at it and let it lie. He looked round and saw me watching him, and smiled, a sad sort of smile. He was big, and red, and baffled silly by Peaches, and I guess he'd been the villain or the clown in all this business, depending on your point of view. But in his own area of expertise, I realised—business, and banking, and all that—he was admired and respected. It was strange to think about that.

"After a while Jonathon seemed to pull himself together and suggested they go out to the back terrace to look at the lights on the harbour, and just about everyone wandered out, just to be with the crowd, including Dad. In a few minutes the room was almost empty. There was just me, by the curtains, and Peaches and William, like two pieces of driftwood left behind by the tide, looking at each other across the carpet. It was a long, slow look. They didn't say anything. Their faces didn't move. They just looked. Then Peaches moved her eyes away, and saw me. She came over to me, and put her hand on my shoulder, and started talking to me, and asking how I was. When I checked again, William had gone.

"I thought Peaches was a bit of a dill, all things considered, and we didn't have much to say to each other. But she did try, and before she went out to join the others, she said to make myself at home—get a book to read from the shelf, if I liked, have some nice things to eat, and all that. So after she was gone I did.

"The food was really good—most of it, anyway—but I didn't enjoy it. I was too nervous. I spilt a bit of Coke on the beautiful white tablecloth. That was the first disaster. Then when I tried to pick a piece of fruit from William's tree, the whole thing tilted right over and a few fruits bounced off, and one broke, so I had to eat it without even having the fun of choosing which one to have. And then while I was trying to get the fruit back on and balance the tree again, I heard people coming back, and I went into a complete panic and dropped the mince pie I was holding in my other hand and trod on it, so it squashed all over the carpet. It was quite awful. It's terrible what kids go through sometimes.

"Anyway, I needn't have worried because they were all so merry by now that they either didn't notice a thing or didn't care. I was just starting to relax and move quietly away from the table back to Dad, when Mrs. Brin came over and smiled at me.

" 'I'm going to be naughty and have my little kiwi fruit now,' she said. 'I swore this year I'd resist, but I just can't.' She bent over to William's tree and looked carefully at the branches. 'Oh, there it is,' she said, and picked the kiwi fruit off. 'Isn't it gorgeous? But so fattening!' And she bit into it.

" 'Oh, I knew you'd have it in the end, Joan,' said Peaches, laughing behind her. 'You always do!'

" 'Well, William does make it just for me,' said Mrs. Brin. 'I wouldn't want to hurt his feelings.'

"I must have stared at them a bit too obviously, because Peaches smiled at me and said I probably thought they were all very childish, but William always brought a different piece of marzipan fruit for every person. Kiwi fruit for Mrs. Brin, because she was a New Zealander, and a peach for her, because of her name, and a bunch of grapes for Mr. Marlow, because he had a vineyard, and so on. I went cold, of course. I'd had no idea. Heaven knew what fruit I was *supposed* to have eaten. It was very unlikely I'd had the right one, anyway. I was incredibly embarrassed, and just scuttled away to Dad without saying anything. And after that the whole thing was a complete misery for me. I just kept watching people going up and carefully choosing their fruit off that little tree, winking red, green, white at me under the fairy lights like a sign of doom, waiting for the moment when someone would fail to find their right and proper sweetie.

"After about half an hour, Jonathon went over to the tree, and I held my breath. I just knew this was it! I watched, fascinated, and waited for him to turn around and say something. But he picked a fruit off the top of the tree without hesitation, bit into it, turned back to the party, and swallowed.

"And then all hell broke loose. Jonathon suddenly looked incredibly horrified, and grabbed at his neck. Then he fell down on the floor. Dr. Beddoes rushed over to him. Everyone crowded around and tried to help, like they do, but he'd been dead as a doornail for fifteen minutes by the time the ambulance came.

"Sweet William kept talking about a heart attack, and Peaches was crying, and as white as chalk. It was strange to see how everyone else reacted. It was an awful social dilemma, after all. How does one behave when one's host has died violently before one's eyes after just having eaten confectionery supplied by a guest who is madly in love with the host's wife? I mean, does one go along with the heart attack theory and go on relating to the guest in question as if the nasty thought of murder had never occurred to one? Most people solved the problem eventually by flocking around and comforting little Peaches, and making her cups of tea and so on. With her as the object of attention, they didn't have to worry about how to treat William.

"The police came, of course. They looked at Jonathon, and smelt his mouth, and looked at the piece of marzipan still in his hand, and sniffed that, and put it in a plastic bag. Peaches watched them, looking shattered and clinging onto Dr. Beddoes' arm for dear life. When she heard the word cyanide, she screamed and hid her face in Dr. Beddoes' shoulder. And when William came up and tried to say something to her she just whispered, 'Why?' and twisted away from him. And then she fainted.

"They took William away, of course, and Jonathon's body, and the sugar tree, as evidence, and the next day, which was Christmas, we heard bits and pieces about what happened then. Peaches had had to go to hospital. She was in shock, they said, and couldn't be interviewed for a day or two. Dr. Beddoes fixed that for her, Dad said. Dad had never had much time for Peaches, really. The police found the pieces of what had been a glass bottle containing cyanide at the bottom of the garbage tin at the back of

Sweet William's shop, and a packed bag in his house. People told the police about William loving Peaches, and how Peaches had clung to Jonathon's arm at the party, and how they'd thought the whole affair was going to boil over any minute one way or another, and generally had a field day. It was a very exciting Christmas.

"So, that was that. At least, everyone thought so. But I was . . . I don't know . . . unsatisfied. It all seemed so pat. And there was something else. I worried about it for a while, and then I went and talked to Dad. I worked up to it gradually. First, just to make absolutely sure I wasn't making a fool of myself, I asked him which marzipan fruit Dr. Beddoes always had. He stared at me as though I was crazy, of course, but then he thought about it, and told me it was the pineapple, because Dr. Beddoes came from Queensland. So then I knew I was right, and I told him what I'd been thinking about, and he stared at me again, for a long time. And then—I took it for granted at the time, I think, but since then I've really admired him for it—Dad called the cops. Most parents would have just told me to run away and play and stop thinking about nasty things. But he didn't.

"And the cops listened too. Maybe it had seemed too pat for them, as well. Anyway, they went to the Macguires' house and searched it with a fine-tooth comb, and found what I'd said they would. Then they went and got past Dr. Beddoes, and had a word with Peaches. Then they talked to the girl who helped Sweet William in the shop. And they looked carefully again at the marzipan Jonathon had been holding when he died. And they found out the truth, thanks to me, I'm delighted to say. So now you know."

"What do you mean, 'Now I know'?" Toby demanded. "What do I know?"

Birdie stretched and yawned. "Well, whodunnit, of course."

"Not Sweet William, I presume?" said Toby drily.

"Of course not. Sweet William was set up, wasn't he? As if

he'd have killed Jonathon as obviously as that! He wasn't a complete idiot."

"Birdwood, I'll kill you if you don't stop this Hercule Poirot business. Spit it out!"

"Dan, the beer must've made you sleepy. It's so obvious I'm embarrassed to tell you. William's nerves, Peaches clinging to Jonathon, the fairy lights, the fruits all earmarked for certain people according to their name, or their profession, or where they came from, my accident with the tree, William's packed bag, Dr. Beddoes having the pineapple— No, don't get up, Dan, I'll tell you."

"Get on with it, then. Just tell me who killed Jonathon Macguire," demanded Toby, who was at this point beyond pretending he didn't care. He sat down again.

Birdie shrugged. "Well, in one way, I did," she said calmly. "*What?*"

"When I knocked the sugar tree over, a few fruits came off. One broke, and I had to eat it. It was an apple. Later I found out that every fruit was specially intended for one person, and I was embarrassed, because I was sure the apple hadn't been intended for me. The only two people I could think of who it could have been for were Dr. Beddoes, because of an apple a day keeping the doctor away, which would have been just typical of William's whimsy, or Jonathon, because of his name. Dad eliminated Dr. Beddoes for me, and then confirmed that the apple was always brought for Jonathon.

"Okay, so I had eaten Jonathon's fruit. So whichever fruit had killed him wasn't his. He ate someone else's by mistake. He wasn't the intended victim at all. Jonathon was a bit drunk, like everyone else, but he wasn't so drunk he'd make a very obvious mistake. I saw him pick a fruit from near the top of the tree. The fairy lights were shining there, and they lit the tree with red and green. I saw it. They coloured the big round fruit Jonathon chose a rosy red, like an apple, and he'd eaten half of it before he turned around to the ordinary light and discovered his mistake. It wasn't an apple, it was a peach. A big, round peach, the peach he'd thought would kill his wife and put her lover in gaol for life.

"He'd substituted the fruit he'd injected with cyanide for the one William brought, you see. The bitter almonds smell of cyanide would be perfectly disguised in marzipan. William's shop assistant remembered him buying three peaches the day before the party, two extra for practice, one presumes—he was a sensible thorough man—and when he was finished with the cyanide he pushed the container into William's bin. He knew it wouldn't be emptied till after Christmas, and that the bottle would still be there when the cops went looking. At the party I saw him hovering at the supper table. He must have done the substitution then. He put the harmless peach in his pocket, and threw it over the deck at the back, when they went out to look at the view. The police found it in the garden."

"Birdie, this can't be right," fretted Toby. "The man would have known exactly where the bloody poisoned bit of fruit was. And his own, probably. It wouldn't matter how many red lights were shining on that bloody peach. He knew where he put it."

"Ah, yes, Dan, but you've forgotten that I knocked the tree over and put the fruit back wherever I could and as quickly as I could. They were all mixed up. But no one knew I'd done that. Jonathon didn't know. So he died."

Toby shook his head. "Poor bugger," he said. "Poor old bugger."

Birdie grinned at him. "I like the way you sympathise with him, Detective Sergeant, I must say. He tried to kill his wife, you know. If it hadn't been for my butter-fingers, he would have succeeded. He'd got a detective onto her. He'd found out she was seeing William on the side, and that they were planning to go off quietly together early on Christmas morning, while Jonathon was sleeping off the party. She told the cops all about it, once they got to her. That's why William had his bag packed, and she was clinging onto Jonathon, at the party, to put him off the scent. They were both terrified of Jonathon."

"I suppose they went off and lived happily ever after, then?" asked Toby sourly. He drained his lukewarm beer.

"Oh, for a while," grinned Birdie, remembering. "But Sweet William was a real romantic, far better at adoring from afar than loving at close quarters. So after about a year of living with Peaches, who had a very sweet tooth and quite soon got rather plump on his cooking, he started mooning over a woman who came into the shop, a dark, thin, mysterious woman, and rather older than him. They disappeared together about six months later. Peaches more or less took to her bed after that, but eventually she recovered and married Dr. Beddoes, who had always fancied her, and had a very reassuring bedside manner."

Toby laughed. "I like that," he said. "That's a good ending."

Birdie looked at her watch. "It's Christmas Day," she said. "Merry Christmas."

"Merry Christmas, mate. God bless us every one," said Dan Toby, and meant it.

RABBIT KILLER

THE HOUSE STOOD RIGHT on top of the hill, and lank, green grass grew all around it, right up to the wormy wooden posts that hitched it slightly from the ground. The house was old, and grey, and when the wind blew the tin roof cracked ominously and the windows rattled. Sometimes the cows wandered up the hill to the house from the paddocks below and stood chewing at the fence, looking into the verandah with melting, incurious eyes. Sometimes the mist came rolling up from the valley and surrounded the house so that it was transformed and silent, and the people inside would gather on the verandah and look out, talking to each other in murmuring voices as if they were in a church, or children were sleeping.

But there were no children in the house now. Hadn't been since Bradley and Bob Winn were boys together, roaming the paddocks, fishing for eels in the creek, skulking under the tank-stand or in the old fig tree by the chicken house to escape their chores and homework, while their mother Jean, thin and crack-

ling with fury in a mauve floral frock, squinted against the sun
from the verandah, and shrilled for them to come to her.

Bradley and Bob were grown men now. Bradley was big, fair
and freckled, like his father had been, and his mild blue eyes had
faded into pale bluish grey. Bob was tall too, but he was thin, dark
and rangy, and his chin was always shadowed, no matter how
closely he shaved. His black eyes were watchful and his long,
brown fingers restless.

They still lived in the old house, the Winn boys. And with
them lived their mother, and Bradley's wife, Shirley. Jean was
older now, and losing her physical strength, but spiritually she
still dominated the house, and the people in it, as comprehen-
sively as she used to do when she could outrun a ten-year-old boy
and drag him back to the house by his collar, flailing at his legs
with a switch the whole way and never drawing breath as she
scolded. She'd been a widow for over twenty years. People of ill
will in the neighbourhood said Frank Winn was so exhausted by
thirty years of living with his wife that he gave in to death gladly
at the first opportunity. Frank was a big man, as his sons were to
be after him, but it was true that Jean, half his size and a quarter
of his weight, had him beat.

People said, "Like father, like son," when Bradley Winn, the
younger of the two brothers, had married a woman as close in
looks and temperament to his mother as one would think possible.
Like Jean, Shirley Williams had lived in the valley all her life.
She'd grown up a few kilometres down the road from the Winn
boys. They were ten and twelve when she was born, and regarded
her with amused tolerance as she grew from the silent, watchful
toddler who shadowed them remorselessly whenever the families
got together to the skinny, freckle-faced teenager who averted her
eyes from them, twisting her handkerchief, as she leaned against
the wall at dances and parties. But in the brief, fragile flowering of
her early twenties, Bradley Winn, thirty-two and growing bored

and restless in his bachelorhood, had opened his mild blue eyes and seen that she was beautiful, felt a stirring he thought must be love, and asked her to marry him.

Possibly she would have preferred Bob, but Bob hadn't asked her, and she knew instinctively that the time was right to secure a mate. So she said yes to Bradley, and moved into the old house on the top of the hill with him, and Bob, and their mother. She was happy to do this. She was used to the house, and liked it. The view was good, and the air was fresher up on the hill than down in the valley where her parents' house crouched by the road and dust, petrol fumes and the sweet, heavy smell of cow pats hung all day inside the dim, vine-draped verandah. The old lady couldn't last forever, and Bob wasn't going to stay, once she went. Then the house would be Shirley's. And Bradley's, of course. And after them, their sons'. In the first months after their marriage, looking at Bradley pulling off his boots at the door, coming to her with his big, flushed face softened and embarrassed by their new relationship, she found, thinking of these things, a tenderness in herself she had never before experienced.

But there were no sons, or daughters either. Just two terrifying, desperate rushes to the local hospital and two sad little bundles, delivered too early, without hope of life, buried in the cemetery outside the town. Shirley had called it quits, then. She let the new, soft place in her heart close over, accepted the hand fate had dealt her without the appearance of pain, and got on with her work as she'd always done. She was a brave little woman, people said, and a wonderful worker. A good wife, too. Bradley was always spotless, the women said, as though he was a baby and needed careful supervision to ensure his face was clean and the folds of his neck free of fluff and crumbs.

So the years went by and one day was very like the next except for the changes in the seasons, marked most notably for the four people in the house by the life cycle of the cattle whose gentle births and bloody, terrified deaths put food on their table, and clothes on their backs. But there were changes. As Jean grew older and frailer, Shirley gradually shouldered more and more of the work of the house. She washed the clothes, mended, cooked and cleaned. She rose first, went to bed last. She was tireless, and accepted no assistance. At night, still wearing her apron, she would draw a stool up to the end of the big table and nibble at the scrappy bits of food left after serving the other three with the good, hot meals she'd cooked. They knew better than to remark on this, or urge her to do otherwise. She grew stronger and stronger as her mother-in-law weakened. She lived like a servant, yet she dominated all their lives by her service, her martyrdom, the shrillness of her voice and her thin-lipped, stony disapproval of anything she saw as wrongdoing or disrespect.

The men worked the farm, separately and together, like their father before them. If Bradley was disappointed or Bob displeased by the life they led, they showed no sign of it. Their growing silence could have been simply the natural result of their work, and the passing of the years, for after all they were used to their harness, even if the hands that held the reins had changed.

Jean Winn, now nearly eighty, grew silent too. She stopped trying to boss her sons and snipe at her daughter-in-law and spent more time sitting on the verandah looking down into the valley. She had surrendered, but showed no signs of dying, and sometimes Shirley thought she never would.

One autumn Bob went to Sydney to the Show and stayed a fortnight instead of his usual week. He returned, even more taciturn than before, with a new sports jacket and a new pair of shoes. After that, at regular intervals, he'd disappear for days at a time to the city—"for a break," he said. Shirley wondered sometimes what the attraction was, and one night, when Jean had gone to bed and she was ironing and Bradley was watching TV, she idly wondered it out loud. She didn't really expect an answer. They didn't talk much, she and Bradley, these days. But he turned from the set and looked at her in slow surprise.

"A woman. He's got a woman there," he said, as if it was obvious.

She felt a sudden stab of shocked jealousy, so violent that she gasped, and her hand went to her heart. She was astonished at herself, and frightened by the strength of the feeling. "*Bob?*" she heard herself shrill. She laughed hoarsely.

"Why not?" her husband said calmly. "I thought you knew." He turned back to the TV set and she stared at the back of his head as if she'd never seen it before.

"Who is it?" She forced herself to speak calmly.

"I dunno. Some woman." Bradley bent to turn the volume up a fraction. "He's keen, anyhow. He'll marry her, if you ask me."

Shirley clenched and twisted her hands on the iron handle, burning her knuckles on the hot metal sides. "Why would he want to do that?"

He turned to look at her again, crouched thin and grimfaced over the ironing board, and a strange expression crossed his face. But he said nothing, and she quickly shrugged and bent again to the shirt she had creased under the iron. The wind blew around the house, rattling the windows and cracking at the tin roof. Old Jean mumbled in her fitful sleep, in the bed she'd shared with her big, snoring husband, and now had all to herself. The cattle bellowed for their calves in the valley. Shirley ironed, fast and expertly, smoothing out the wrinkle she had made. Everything was as it always was. But nothing would ever be the same again.

"It was awfully nice of you to come, Birdie. I feel much better now you're here." Marion Moore fluttered in her armchair.

Verity Birdwood, gratefully absorbing a cool glass of beer, nodded briefly in reply and thought how like her mother Marion was growing. That kind, worried face—even the prim hairstyle—reminded her of long-ago school speech days, and Mrs. Moore in a blue dress, smiling with pride as Marion took out, yet again, the good conduct prize for her year, and occasionally a cup for tennis.

"Davey's relieved, too. He doesn't talk about it much, but I know he is relieved," Marion chattered on. Her fingers plucked at her skirt. "I know you don't know him, Birdie. He couldn't . . . I mean, Mum never brought him up to Sydney when she came, but I've told him all about you, and how clever you are at solving crimes and everything, and he's really looking forward to meeting you."

Birdie felt uncomfortable. She'd responded to Marion's phone call on a whim. She'd been bored, and she'd remembered Marion as one of the few girls at school who'd always been pleasant and inoffensive. Not one of Birdie's particular friends, no great brain, certainly, but a nice girl. She'd rarely talked about her brother Davey at school. While other girls chattered and complained about their various siblings' faults and achievements, Marion had been silent, and everyone knew that this was because her brother was "mentally retarded"—a phrase always whispered in fear and awe, and never in front of Marion.

After the final exams Marion had disappeared back to the country and Birdie hadn't thought of her again, except for one brief meeting at a school reunion ten years ago during which it became obvious that, because of the illness of their mother and the death of their father, Davey had become his sister's responsibility. But it seemed that Marion had kept the memory of her schooldays fresh in her mind. A couple of years before, she had seen a small paragraph in the paper naming her old acquaintance as having been of assistance to the police in a particularly sensational murder case. She had pointed it out to her husband and her brother, and had clipped it out to keep. And when she needed help of a very particular kind, she remembered. Now her brother was in trouble, and Marion, with her usual expectation that every-one else was as warm-hearted and eager to please as herself, had tracked down Birdie and simply asked her to come.

And Birdie had. Even now she wondered why. The case seemed unfortunately clear-cut, especially once she'd digested the newspaper clippings and information Marion had pressed upon her on her arrival. Davey, a powerful young man with an easy smile and a penchant for Phantom comics and videos of the more basic kind, had been doing odd jobs, as he often did, on a property outside town. One of the women on the place, a little tartar named Shirley Winn, had had words with him shortly after lunch. Something about a fence he was supposed to have fixed, and cows breaking into her vegetable garden behind the house. Her husband, his brother, their mother and the brother's wife had all witnessed the argument.

Afterwards, the brothers had gone out, one to town, one to ride round the cattle. The brother's wife, Julia Winn, a city woman who apparently did little around the place, had gone off to read in one of the front paddocks, under a tree. The mother, who was very old, had been put to bed as usual for her afternoon sleep. The two men saw Davey Moore down by the broken fence as they left. He seemed to be mending it as he'd been told to do, but was working slowly and continually glanced up towards the house, where Shirley Winn was pegging clothes on the line in the side yard. Her body had been discovered by her husband at dusk, hidden under the huge pumpkin vine that grew just above the vegetable patch. Her neck had been broken by a massive blow to the nape. She'd died instantly, the doctor had said. Probably never knew what hit her. Cattle were grazing around her, tram-pling the vine, crushing and tearing at the young cabbages. The hole in the fence gaped unmended. Davey Moore was gone.

"They've never even looked for any other solution, you know, Birdie," Marion whispered. "Just because Davey was there, and she'd had words with him, and he's . . . like he is, you know, they just fixed it on him. But he wouldn't have done it, Birdie, no matter what she said to him. He's the gentlest boy—the gentlest."

"Marion, I've read all the stuff you gave me," said Birdie slowly, "but I think you'll have to face it that Davey was angry with the woman, was there alone with her round the time of her death, and . . ." She hesitated, not wanting to completely quench the hope in Marion's mild eyes, but then went on resolutely. No point in giving her any false hope. ". . . and he had a weapon."

"They never found any piece of fence post or tool with blood or hair or anything on it, Birdie! They didn't! They looked."

"He could have just thrown it away on his way home to you, Marion," Birdie pointed out. "And anyway, the cops seemed to think that he could've, well, done it without—"

"Oh, that stupid karate business you mean!" Marion wrung her hands feverishly. "Birdie, that's all such nonsense! He just watches these stupid videos, and pretends—"

"The cops claimed he practised breaking wood with his hands. He's been seen doing it. He has calluses."

Marion flushed and her eyes began to brim over. "He's just pretending! He's like a little child in most ways, Birdie. He'd never use it on a person." She wiped her eyes and took a deep breath. "Just once," she went on, biting at her bottom lip and staring straight ahead, "just once, he . . . he killed a rabbit, you know, by hitting it behind the head, like that." She brought the side of her own hand down sharply on the arm of her chair, then stared at it in horror and quickly curled the fingers. "But the rabbit was dying, had myxomatosis. It was in awful pain, Birdie, when we found it, couldn't run away from these kids who'd got to it, poking and prodding at it with sticks, poor thing. And I told Davey to kill it, to put it out of its misery. He did it. He always does what I tell him. But he hated it. He was upset for weeks. And those silly little boys who saw it, calling him 'rabbit killer' afterwards, and screaming and running away from him in the street as if they were scared. They were just tormenting him, playing the fool. Kids can be so cruel. They know he's not . . . right, and they just like to torture him, like they liked torturing the rabbit. I couldn't believe it when the police started asking him about it." She ran down at last, took another shuddering breath, and slumped back in her chair, her handkerchief clutched to her mouth.

Birdie looked at her in silence for a moment. "They haven't actually arrested him, have they, Marion?" she said at last.

"No. But they're going to. They've had him down at the station lots of times, and I've seen them watching the house—to make sure he doesn't try to run away, I'm sure. As if he would. Where would he go? They're sure it's him. I can see it. But they've got to be careful, because he's . . . like he is. They're moving slowly. Mr. Mackie, our solicitor you know, is doing his best, but honestly, Birdie, even I can see he hasn't got the faintest chance of actually doing anything. He's never ever been involved in anything like this. And anyway, I think *he* thinks Davey did it, too. Everyone does. Everyone except me. I'm all he's got. And you're all *I've* got. Do you see?"

Birdie nodded. She did see. "I'll do what I can, Marion. But I've got no authority to see any evidence or anything like that, and I've absolutely got to get back to Sydney by Monday morning. I mightn't be able to do much."

"Just what you can, Birdie. I understand. Mr. Mackie has organised for you to go out to the house, anyway. He knows the Winns really well. Bob Winn said you could go out there and have a look around this afternoon."

"Well, that's something." Birdie put down her glass,

stretched, and suddenly grinned at Marion. "We'll give it a go. Let me talk to Davey now, and get the ball rolling."

Under Marion's anxious, hopeful eye it had been difficult to sound anything but reassuring and optimistic, but the sight of Davey, dark, chunky and muscular in his checked shirt, casually thumping the pillow on his rumpled bed while he watched *Rocky III* with absorbed concentration, did nothing to make Birdie feel encouraged.

He sat up when Marion spoke to him, though, and smiled at Birdie. A sweet, slow smile. She sat down on the edge of the bed and began asking him questions which he answered carefully, sometimes repeating himself, to make sure she'd understood. He spoke like a small boy—Marion had said that his mental age was about eight—and his hazel eyes were guileless as they fixed on Birdie's own, occasionally sliding away to catch the images on the screen that still flickered, though Marion had turned the sound down.

His story was simple. Mrs. Winn, Shirley Winn, had got after him for not mending the vegetable garden fence early in the day, as he'd been asked to do. He'd said he couldn't, because he couldn't find the big pliers he needed to twist the wire and pull it tight.

"She said they were on the shelf in the shed, but they weren't. She said I was an idiot and no good as a helper. She said Bradley was a half-wit to give me jobs, and she was sick of half-wits round the place." His big hands clenched in his lap. "She was really angry and rude, Marion." He looked at his sister, frowning.

"Never mind, Davey," crooned Marion, and looked worriedly at Birdie. "You just tell Birdie what happened then."

"Then Bradley told her to lay off me. He looked really angry too. And she told him to mind his own business. And Bob said, 'Calm down, Shirley,' but she never said anything to him." He fell silent. His eyes slid once more to the TV screen.

"Finish the story now, Davey," prompted Marion gently.

"I forget the rest." He hunched his shoulders irritably. "Can't I watch my movie?"

"Just a little bit longer, Davey." Birdie put her hand on his arm to attract his attention. He turned back to her reluctantly and waited. "You went down the back in the end and started to fix the fence, is that right?"

He nodded. "Bob found the pliers," he said. "And they weren't even in the shed, you know. They were in the kitchen. So she'd blamed me for nothing!"

"Right, so Bradley went off on his horse, is that right? You saw him go?"

"Yeah. He waved at me. He was going round the cattle."

"And Bob went to town in the car?"

"No. He went in the ute."

"Oh well, in the ute then. So you saw them both go. Could you see Mrs. Winn? Mrs. Shirley Winn, Bradley's wife?"

Davey's face darkened. "She was hanging out the clothes," he muttered reluctantly. "Old bitch."

"Davey!" exclaimed Marion, stepping forward. But Birdie stared her into silence and turned back to the boy.

"Did you see anyone else?"

"Nup." His eyes strayed once more to the TV screen.

"What about Bob's wife, Davey? Julia, isn't it? Did you see where Julia went?" Birdie persisted, sighing inwardly. This was heavy going.

"Oh, she went before," he said impatiently. "Before I went out to the fence. She went down the front paddock." He grinned suddenly. "Bob really likes Julia. I like her too. She laughs, and she's really pretty."

Marion cast her eyes up. " 'Really pretty' means made-up and dressed to the nines, Birdie. Don't expect a raving beauty. But it's true Bob's as silly as a wheel about her. They've only been married six months. She's a Sydney girl—well, woman, of course. She won't see forty again, whatever she'd like everyone to think."

Birdie's eyebrows shot up. It was just about the first time she'd ever heard Marion being sharp about anyone.

Marion saw her expression, looked confused and laughed shortly to cover her discomfiture. "She gets on my nerves, Julia Winn. What did she marry a farmer for, if she was going to pine for town every minute of the day? Mind you, that house wouldn't be my cup of tea, and as for living with Shirley and Brad and old mum Winn, well . . ." She cast up her eyes again.

"Sounds delightful," laughed Birdie. She smiled at Davey, who was looking at them in bewilderment. "So then what did you do, Davey?" she asked casually.

He hunched his shoulders and, for the first time, looked shifty. "I didn't want to stay there," he mumbled, looking sideways at Marion. "I didn't want to fix her stupid fence. So I come home."

"You walked?" asked Birdie. "But it's an awfully long way, isn't it?" She looked enquiringly at Marion.

"Ten kilometres, about," sighed Marion. "Bradley was going to drop him on the highway at the end of the day. That's what usually happens. But you didn't wait for Bradley, did you, Davey? He just downed tools and walked all that way, and got shocking blisters instead. Oh, Davey, why did you do such a silly thing?"

"I didn't want to stay there," repeated Davey stubbornly. "Old bitch."

"Davey!"

. . .

The road that led from the highway to the Winn farm was at first a conventional one but, once safely out of sight behind the first hill, it grew winding and narrow, lost its black sealed surface, became dusty, potholed, eccentric and charming. On either side of it the green country rose to hills and fell away to valleys, and red cattle stood in knots under gum trees, sheltering from the afternoon sun. But Birdie, busy persuading her dilapidated car that it could cope with the road's charm, and reviewing her talk with Davey Moore, was not looking at the view.

She had told Marion that Davey's story was very damaging, combined with the evidence of the other people involved. The dead woman, Shirley Winn, had been hanging out clothes not far from where he was working beside the vegetable patch. There was no one to see except the old lady, and she was asleep in her room. Davey obviously still held a grudge against Shirley, even now. How much stronger must his anger and resentment have been then? Did he brood on her unfairness and unpleasantness as he crouched by the fence, looking up through the vegetable patch at her skinny arms hanging out the clothes? Did he decide, quite suddenly and simply, that the world would be a better place without her? Did he creep up behind her, as she bent over the clothes basket, for example, and dispatch her with one of those "rabbit killer" punches to the neck Birdie herself had seen him practising in his bedroom? Then, terrified by what he had done, did he hide the body in the pumpkin vine and take off for home, Marion and sanctuary, while the cattle moved slowly in through the hole in the fence to obliterate the traces of the attack?

It could have happened that way. It was, in fact, the simplest and most likely thing to have happened, and Birdie had told Marion so, quietly and firmly, when they had left Davey's room. The guilelessness of Davey's hazel eyes did not affect Birdie's opinion on this. Marion had said he wouldn't lie, because he was mentally a child, but in Birdie's experience eight-year-old boys were cunning and manipulative as sin, and the more angelic they looked, the more one should watch one's back. She'd told Marion it seemed to her extremely unlikely that she could find for the police a solution that would satisfy them more. But Marion's faith that her old schoolfriend could help save her brother was as strong as it was unrealistic and typical of her, and her faith in her brother's innocence was of the same order.

Birdie hunched over the wheel, peering at the road ahead and cursing the dust and the hairpin bends. Over a little bridge, Marion had said, then past a white house on your left, up a rise, past a big fig tree and there was the Winn gate on your right, with a big yellow mailbox to mark the spot. She craned her neck, looking for splashes of yellow. Curiosity was driving her, she realised. Just go and see them, Marion had said when Birdie, fidgeting, told her she thought it was a waste of time to go out to the Winn farm. "You'll see. You'll see why I don't believe Davey did it. Why should it be him, a stranger, when there are other much more likely propositions right there in the family?" But she'd say no more than that. She was smarter than she looked, Marion. At that moment Birdie drove into the black shade of a huge old fig that canopied the road. She blinked. It was as though the sun had been put out. The Winn gate stood a few metres ahead, in deep shadow. From it a track climbed up to an old, grey house on the very top of a steep little hill. The house had a curiously isolated and grim look to it. There were people moving about there, and a couple of cars parked. The Winns were at home, and waiting for her.

The four of them sat with her around the big table in the dead centre of the main room of the house. Bradley, the widower, hunched at the end, his features blurred with grief or confusion. His mother sat beside him, belligerent, tiny and infinitely wrinkled, her bony hands, scarred by decades of work in the service of farm and family, clasped before her. On the other side of the table sat the dark older brother, Bob, and his new wife, the Julia Winn that Marion had spoken about with such uncharacteristic asperity. Birdie could see why. Julia would always rouse a measure of animosity in the women she dealt with. She was a man's woman, lighting up in male company, and seeing women as no company at all. She radiated confidence, confidence verging on utter complacency. She was big—almost as tall as Bob and heavily built with it, but she showed no sign of being diffident about the fact. On the contrary, her glamorous, unsuitable clothes and jewellery were designed to attract attention, and her beautifully made-up face was alive with the awareness of her own appeal. In a corner a clock ticked. Cups rattled on saucers as afternoon tea, weak and black, was politely drunk.

"You're a friend of Marion Moore's," said Bob Winn at last, with an air of getting down to unavoidable, unpleasant business. His voice was casual, but his manner was watchful, and as he spoke his eyes darted across to his brother.

Birdie nodded. "We went to school together," she said. "I'm a solicitor. She thought I might be able to help."

"You're welcome to look around," Bradley rumbled, big and freckled at the end of the table. "We said to Tom Mackie you were. We want to do the right thing by Marion, whatever Davey Moore's done. But I can't see the point, frankly. They've been through the lot already, the cops have. Nothing to see." He looked at her under his eyebrows. His eyes were tired and strained-looking, and his blunt hands fumbled together on the tabletop.

"I don't know if I can help, and I'm really sorry to disturb you like this," said Birdie, in her most diffident manner. "But I told Marion I'd do what I can. She's sure Davey wouldn't hurt anyone."

"Well, she would be, wouldn't she?" Julia Winn spoke matter-of-factly from her place beside the teapot. She raised her black, arched eyebrows as everyone looked at her, and Jean Winn snorted contemptuously. "It's only natural, surely," she persisted, blandly eyeing her mother-in-law.

"Davey Moore wouldn't hurt a fly," Jean replied repressively. "Anyone with half a brain could see that. The police won't fall for that one."

Julia gave a small smile, and shrugged, glancing at her husband.

"The trouble is, Mum, if Davey didn't do it, who did?" he said gently.

The old woman cackled and waved her skinny hand around the table. "Take your pick!" she shrilled, and laughed again.

There was a shocked silence. Birdie dropped her eyes and tried to control her mouth. There was really nothing funny about this.

"If I could just ask you a few questions?" she said gravely. "About—that afternoon. It's possible someone else came here that day. Someone none of you knows about."

Julia shook her head. "I'd have seen them," she said, rather loudly. "I was reading, down there in that clump of trees, the whole afternoon." She gestured vaguely towards the front of the house where the green hill slid away past a clump of trees and a dam, to the road. "I saw a few cars pass, and they saw me, because of my red sunhat, you know, but no one drove up to the house."

"Someone could have come on foot," Birdie suggested.

"I would have seen them," the woman repeated stubbornly.

"Did you see Davey leave?"

She hesitated. "Well, no, I didn't," she admitted reluctantly.

"I didn't. But he probably slipped out through one of the fences on the other side of the hill. Through Thorson's place, Bob." She appealed to her husband.

He nodded. "Very likely. Davey knows this area like the back of his hand, Miss . . . ah . . . He probably did go out through our neighbour's place. You ask him."

"Fred Thorson still on about buying this place, is he, Bob?" the old lady put in abruptly.

Her older son looked uncomfortable, and again darted a quick glance at his brother. But Bradley remained silent, staring at his fists on the tabletop. "Don't you worry about that, now, Mum," Bob murmured. "We'll see."

"You're going to sell, aren't you?" she accused, fixing the two of them with a darting black eye. "Now Shirley's out of the way there's no one to stand against you. I can't fight you, can I? A feeble old woman, a burden on all of you."

"Mum!" the two men began, with embarrassed looks at Birdie. But Julia put her elaborately manicured hand on the old lady's arm.

"It would be much the best thing for all of us, Jean," she said reasonably. "The place isn't paying anymore, you know that. These days you need a place twice the size. That's why Fred Thorson wants to expand. And why he's offering so much. With the money he's offering, Brad and Bob could buy that agency they want. And we could get a place in town. And you could have a few comforts, instead of roughing it out here. You'd like it, really you would."

"Is that so?" demanded Jean, struggling to rise to her feet. "I know all about your 'place in town.' You'll dump me back in that hospital, won't you? With all those nurses fussing over me and whatnot? I know. Well, you'll do what you like. I can't stop you. And Shirley can't stop you. Not anymore. No, look, leave me alone, can't you? I don't want to lie down. I don't need it!"

With a resigned shrug, Julia had firmly taken the old lady's arm. Ignoring her protestations she guided her to a bedroom at the back of the house.

"Mum's not well," Bob said, looking Birdie straight in the eye, as if daring her to comment on the scene she'd just witnessed. "She broke her hip a while ago, and had to go to hospital. She was there for weeks, and hasn't really come good yet. Needs a lot of looking after."

"Shirley used to look after her like a baby," muttered Bradley, almost to himself. He set his strong jaw. "She was wonderful to Mum. She knew how Mum felt about this place. Remember, Bob, how she'd say to her, 'Don't you worry, Mum Winn, they'll never sell this place out from under you while I'm here to stop them'? Remember that, Bob?"

"How could I forget?" said Bob drily, and rattled his teacup warningly. But Bradley would not be deflected.

" 'No way I'm going to let them put you back into that place,' Shirley said, when Mum come home from hospital. 'Don't you worry yourself about that,' she said. 'I'm here and I'll see you end your days here where you belong, if I have to work my fingers to the bone . . .' " His big face began to crumple. "And now . . . now Shirl's gone and we're, we're . . ."

"Pull yourself together, mate," growled Bob, not unkindly. He pushed his chair away from the table, fixed the fascinated Birdie with a dark stare and jerked his head towards the verandah. She rose obediently and followed him into the fresh air.

"He's upset," Bob said unnecessarily, then fell silent and gazed out at the paddocks falling away from them into the valley. Birdie felt a movement behind her, turned and jumped slightly to see Julia there. She had moved very quietly for such a tall woman. She was shaking her head in mock frustration, smiling broadly.

"That old lady is cunning as a fox, you know," she laughed. "She absolutely loves her afternoon sleep, but she won't admit it.

Needs to play this game that she's being made to do it. That way, you see," she added, nodding at Birdie, "she gets to be the hard-working, gallant little martyr and have her lazy afternoon as well! Talk about having your cake and eating it too!"

"Ah, Julia!" remonstrated Bob, his face relaxing into a half-guilty smile. He was obviously delighted with his wife. Birdie could see why. She must have been a breath of fresh air to a man nurtured on female joylessness and self-sacrifice. For all her inappropriately careful grooming and brashness, there was an insouciance about Julia that was very attractive, especially in these surroundings.

"She'll love it in town, Bob," Julia went on breezily. "Believe me, she will! Whether she lives with us or—somewhere else. Heavens, that stay in hospital was the best thing that ever happened to her, if you ask me. Comfortable bed, air-conditioning, good food, her own TV, nice view, lots of people to pick on . . . bliss!"

"Ah, Julia," protested Bob again, but again he smiled. She put her hand to his cheek, and Birdie saw the hard muscle relax under smooth, white fingers. "And we've got ourselves to think of, too, haven't we?" she said brightly.

"Maybe." He spoke gruffly, hitching at his belt and squinting past her at the road, but her lips curved as she dropped her hand. She would get her way, thought Birdie.

Julia turned to look at her, and her smile broadened. "Will I give you the grand tour, Verity? Or would you rather poke around unaccompanied?"

"A bit of both, if that's okay," said Birdie casually.

"Sure. See you later, darling." She laid a hand on Bob's arm. "Don't work too hard."

He ducked his head in response, and mumbled something as she led Birdie back inside. Bradley had disappeared from his place at the end of the table. Muffled snoring sounds drifted from

Jean's bedroom. The dim, deserted living room smelt of old wood and the dust between the floorboards, and a fly buzzed drearily. Julia waved her hand around and rolled her eyes. "Depressing, isn't it? Oh, I'll be so glad to get out of here, you've got no idea!"

"It's got atmosphere," Birdie ventured.

Julia laughed softly. "It's got that, all right," she whispered. "Much more than its share. Anyway . . ."

She led Birdie to a door at the side of the living room where hats hung on hooks above a double row of boots. She pulled down a new-looking wide-brimmed red straw hat and clapped it on her head. "You should wear one if we're going out," she said, glancing pointedly at Birdie's pale face. "Like one of these for now? Sorry, they're not very glam."

Birdie looked at the selection. They were a bent and scruffy-looking lot. She reached for the one nearest, but Julia casually steered her hand on to the next. "Better not take Shirley's, though," she whispered. "She never had it off her head when she was outside, and if Bradley saw you wandering around in it he might get a bit funny."

"Oh, God, yes." Birdie looked at the grey, tattered piece of moulded straw that had been Shirley Winn's. Why on earth was it still hanging there?

"Bradley hasn't touched a thing of Shirley's," whispered Julia, as if she'd read her thoughts. "Absolutely nothing's been touched since that day. The only things missing are the clothes she was wearing when she was found. The police have them. It's just as if she was still here, right down to her toothbrush in the bathroom, and much as I'd love to, I don't see how I can do anything about it. It's extremely creepy, and another reason why I'll be glad to get out of here. I mean, every time I see that hat I think of Shirley, toiling away out the back, hanging out her ever-lasting washing, all that."

She led the way through the door and out past a very basic

bathroom and laundry, into the side yard of the house. Hens crooned and pecked in a wire enclosure fifty metres away. On an old-fashioned clothesline nearby, a few shirts and a pair of black knickers flapped. Obviously Julia wasn't a great one for big washing days.

At the back of the house, around the corner from the clothesline, the ground fell away steeply from the house. Hot afternoon sun flooded the slope and a neat, terraced vegetable garden. But it was the sprawling pumpkin vine above the prim garden plot and in direct contrast to it, that drew the eye. Julia pointed.

"That's where she was," she said briefly, and watched as Birdie padded down the hill in her soft shoes, trying not to skid on the thick grass that covered the slope.

The pumpkin vine had already almost recovered from the damage caused by the invading cows, and the removal of Shirley Winn's body. Its huge, rough leaves and thick, ridged stalks rose menacingly from the grass it had crushed and yellowed as it grew. Huge blue pumpkins hulked in its depths.

Birdie looked at it curiously. No problem hiding a body there, especially a small one. But why hide the body at all? It was unnecessary and illogical. The hiding place, so near the house, would certainly be discovered fairly quickly, once everyone came home and a search for the missing woman began. Of course, if Davey did the murder, the problem was simple, logical thinking not being his strong suit, and panic-stricken impulse very likely. But if he didn't—if someone else did—what possible reason could they have had for concealing the body? To prevent early discovery and mislead about the *time* of death?

"Okay?" Julia, right behind her, spoke softly, but again made Birdie jump. She had come close without making a sound. She smiled at the startled look, and adjusted her dark glasses. "Sorry, honey. Didn't mean to give you a fright, but I didn't like to shout.

Jean, my mother-in-law, she sleeps very lightly, and she's a fresh air freak so the window has to be open." She pointed back up to the house where lace curtains flapped at an open window against which Birdie could see the cast-iron head of an old double bed.

Birdie nodded thoughtfully. "Could you show me exactly where Davey was mending the fence?"

"Sure." Julia led the way down the steep slope to the vegetable garden, then veered to the left till they reached the wire fence that formed the boundary of the yard. "Just about here, it was. Yes, look—you can see where the new wire's been put in. Bob did it, in the end."

Birdie stood by the fence and looked back up towards the house. This, then, was what Davey had seen that afternoon. It was very similar to what she had imagined. The house reared up on its stumps, blank and plain except for its windows. No sheltering verandah on this side to soften its utilitarian shape. The shirts on the clothesline where Shirley Winn had stood flapped in plain view. On the other side of the house the track that led to the gate could be seen before it dipped to go down the valley. So Bob had waved to Davey on his way to town, and Bradley had waved likewise on his way to "go round the cattle," whatever that meant. But . . .

"You went to read on the other side, down near the road that afternoon, didn't you?" Birdie asked casually. She swatted at a fly on her arm. "Don't the flies bother you?"

Julia laughed. "Of course they do. Drive me insane. But you have to do something, don't you? Can't sit inside all the time."

Birdie shrugged. "I'd have gone to town with the old man, myself."

"Oh, well." Julia turned away with a little laugh. "He had things to do. Can't be hanging round his neck all the time, can I?"

They began walking back to the house. Birdie glanced again

at the open window of the old woman's room. "You know," she said softly, as they passed beneath it, "it's funny your mother-in-law didn't hear anything that day, isn't it? If she's such a light sleeper, and with the window wide open and everything. The murderer was taking an awful risk." She stole a look at Julia's face. It was set and lightly gleaming with sweat over the makeup. Julia brushed impatiently at some flies buzzing around her sunglasses.

"I don't suppose Davey Moore would be too concerned about risk," she said. "He'd be acting on impulse, wouldn't he? And anyway," she added lightly, "as it happened, the window was shut that day."

"Oh, why was that?"

"Well, I don't know, do I?" exclaimed Julia, at last showing a little temper. "I didn't settle her that day. I left it for Shirley to do. I went off to read my book, in fact, just after Shirley'd had a go at Davey. I just left them to it." She turned to Birdie and her dark glasses gleamed in the afternoon sun. "I'd had the lot of them, frankly. My husband included. The flies and cow pats outside were infinitely preferable to one more minute in that dreary, miserable house. And what the hell does it matter, anyway?"

She strode on up the hill, with Birdie padding after her. She swung into the side door of the house, tore off the smart red hat and entered the dimness of the living room. There she seemed to quieten. She took off her sunglasses, slowly put her hat back on the waiting peg and smiled at Birdie ruefully.

"The heat gets me down," she said, and shrugged. It was an apology of sorts. "Look, Jean said Shirley never came in to open the window that afternoon. We usually keep the windows on that side shut, because of the afternoon sun, and we open hers when she goes to have her sleep. She can't manage it herself. Jean said she waited, and called out a few times, but Shirley never came, so she had to go to sleep with it shut. She was bloody cranky about it, too." Her red lips twitched slightly. "The fact that Shirley was probably lying dead under the clothesline while she was lying there fuming doesn't seem to have occurred to her."

Birdie nodded slowly, and hung up her own borrowed hat next to the sad, shapeless straw that had belonged to Shirley Winn. "How long do you reckon you were reading down in the paddock, Julia?" she asked.

"I told the police about an hour and a half," said Julia indifferently. "And I think that's right, because I turned on the radio when I got back, and remember hearing the three-thirty news bulletin."

"Didn't you wonder where Shirley was?"

"No. I was just glad to be on my own for a while. I made a cup of tea and drank it. I suppose I thought she was working in the vegetable garden, if I thought about it at all. It's the sort of thing she loved doing, digging in the heat. Growing huge, tough cabbages you could buy for a few cents, and then stewing them to mush and forcing us to eat them." The rush of words dried up, and a look that might have been shame crossed her face. "Sorry. I forgot for a minute—that she was dead. You must think I'm awful. But I'm not. It's this house. It brings out the worst in me. Look, I'll get us a beer, okay? We'll have it out the front."

Birdie smiled and murmured politely. The house seemed to bring out the worst in all of them, she thought. Now that she'd met them she could understand Marion's fury that the police had looked no further than Davey for a suspect. She walked out onto the verandah and sat down on an old cane chair, kicking at the dusty floorboards with a battered sneaker and gazing down to the roadway threading through the valley below.

The trouble was, all of them had alibis. If the argument occurred at about two o'clock, Shirley must have been hanging out the clothes at, say, two-fifteen to two-thirty. She must have been killed just as she'd finished—at two-thirty or two forty-five, at the latest. Otherwise she would have gone in and put up old Jean's window, as she'd promised.

Bob was on the road to town, then. He'd been seen by several neighbours. He had, fortunately for him, varied his usual taciturn habit by sounding his horn and waving as he passed. He'd actually stopped and talked to one, a Mr. Milne, at the highway turnoff at two-thirty. It was a twenty-minute drive, at least, between the house and the highway. Birdie had taken half an hour to do it. So Bob was washed out.

Bradley went off on his horse at about the same time Bob left. Two boys practising jumping their own horses in a paddock across the road saw him go over the hill and straight down to the knot of cattle grazing by the boundary between the Winn property and the Thorson farm. Fred Thorson and his son were down there working on a new dam, as they'd been every afternoon for a week. They went over to the fence, for a yarn, they said. He didn't usually like to stop during the working day, but that afternoon he seemed a bit fed up and twitchy, and wanted to talk. Trouble with the wife, they reckoned. They gave him a beer from their Esky, and had a good old chat for . . . oh . . . half an hour at least. Then he'd come through the fence and given them a hand for another half hour before going off to his own work. Nice bloke, Bradley Winn. They'd been pleased to see him. Must have been, thought Birdie, since they were trying to talk him into selling his place, and here was a heaven-sent opportunity. Anyway, that was Bradley. Accounted for between two and three, at least. Another washout.

Jean Winn was there in the house all the time. She was the only one with no alibi. But she wouldn't have had the strength to deliver the blow that killed Shirley Winn, and judging by the conversation Birdie had witnessed earlier, she seemed to be the

only one in the house who had an interest in keeping Shirley alive
—unless you counted Bradley, and Birdie wasn't sure you could.

And then there was Julia. Julia was reading halfway down the
hill, a good ten minutes' walk away from the house, at the time
Shirley must have died. According to the notes Marion had given
Birdie, she had been noticed from the road, because of her bright
red hat, by several passing motorists and the boys in the paddock
on the other side of the road. None of these witnesses was particularly certain about exact times, but the boys' testimony made it
clear that they were in the paddock between two and three-fif-
teen, and they'd noticed her sitting there, quite still, the whole
time. Had laughed and commented on it to each other, in fact.
They'd assumed she'd dozed off. Probably couldn't imagine anyone sitting still reading for that long, little yokels, thought Birdie,
grinning to herself. She thought for a moment about that, gazing
across the valley, her eyes behind the thick glasses narrowing in
the silence.

Jean Winn's bedroom was stuffy and hot, despite the open window. The old lady sat up against her pillows, glowering, her short
grey hair standing up in damp tufts. The view through the window was beautiful—green hills and stands of gum trees as far as
the eye could see. But the bed faced into the room, its cast-iron
head jammed firmly against the narrow sill, and Jean's view was a
brown wooden door and a worn, checked dressing-gown hanging
from a hook. It wasn't really a small room, though it gave the
impression of pokiness because the furniture—the bed, cupboard,
dressing table—was massive in the old-fashioned way, and
crowded the available space. Everything was old, from the
patched cover on the bed to the dim framed print of two pine
trees on the wall. The door swung shut behind you, closing you

in, then caught, before it clicked, on uneven floorboards. The window, thick with bubbled varnish, had chocks jammed in the frame to keep it up; the thin rug on the floor wrinkled at the slightest tread. An inconvenient, overcrowded, unpleasant room, Birdie found it. Yet presumably this old woman saw it with different eyes. For her, it was a repository of dreams and memories.

Birdie sat on the edge of the bed and looked at Jean Winn calmly.

"Where is everyone?" demanded the old lady. "I'm parched."

"Julia's making you a cup of tea. I'm just keeping you company till it's ready. I don't know where the others are." Birdie swung her legs gently.

"What do you want?" The question wasn't rude. Just direct. This was a woman with no time or energy to waste.

Birdie turned her head to look out the window. "Could you just tell me if you saw anything, anything at all unusual, from here, the afternoon your daughter-in-law was killed? Did you see Davey Moore working on the fence, for instance?"

Jean Winn tossed her head irritably. "I told the police. I come in here to go to sleep, not look out the window. But I saw Davey Moore, yes. When I was getting into bed I saw him."

"What time would that have been?"

"How would I know? Ten past two or something, I suppose. And I didn't see anyone else. Not a soul. And I didn't hear anything either, because this old devil of a window was shut. That all?"

Birdie said nothing, but stood up and went closer to the window. She bent to look out. The vegetable garden and the fence where Davey had worked were in plain sight. But the clothesline was hidden around the corner of the house.

Jean grunted, heaved herself over and grasped the bedrail,

hauling herself to her knees so that she too could peer out. "What's out there?" she croaked curiously.

Birdie shrugged. "Nothing," she answered briefly. But as she turned back into the room her eyes were thoughtful.

"You saw something!" The old lady was avid now. "What? Go on!" She craned her neck to see.

"I didn't see anything," insisted Birdie truthfully. "Look, do you need help to get down? The tea'll be ready by now."

She helped Jean to sit down and slide her feet to the floor, followed her to the door and ushered her out to the living room and into a chair. Then, murmuring something indistinguishable, she slipped back into the bedroom.

The door swung softly shut behind her. The rug twisted under her hurrying feet. She knelt on the bed and as quietly as she could slipped the chocks from the window frame. They came as easily as she'd hoped, and the window slid down smoothly while she grimly supported its weight to stop it rattling, or banging the sill. Speed was essential, but she didn't want to draw attention to her activities at this point. When it was closed she took a quick look out and, satisfied, heaved the window up again and replaced the chocks carefully. It was heavy all right. A struggle to move even for her.

The doorknob rattled and the door began to open, sticking on the floorboards. Birdie leapt from the bed and smoothed the cover. By the time Julia Winn poked her head into the room she was looking intently out through the open window, her chin on her hand.

"Don't you want your tea? Bob and Bradley are on their way up." Julia sounded bored, but her posture was stiff and her eyebrows arched high. Birdie had a feeling she was outstaying her welcome in this house.

"Coming," she said lightly. "I just wanted to check on something. And the view's so lovely, isn't it?"

"Oh, gorgeous," Julia Winn drily answered, and ushered her from the room.

Birdie felt eyes watching her as she picked her way down the slope towards the stand of trees by the big dam. The urge to look back towards the house was overwhelming, and finally she couldn't resist bending down and taking a peep behind her as she pretended to re-tie her shoelace. They were all standing on the verandah, the two big men with their hands in their pockets, Julia by Bob's side. Old Jean was leaning heavily on the verandah rail, apart from them, gazing out across the valley. Birdie began to whistle softly to herself. The shadows were lengthening now, and the heat was rapidly going out of the air. A car went by on the road below, dust rising behind it. She realised it was the first she'd noticed for quite a while. Soon there would be few passers-by to notice the strange car up at the Winns' place, and once the light went no one would be aware of her visit, except Marion, ten kilometres away and not expecting her at any particular time.

She quickened her pace. If she was right about all this, she would have to tread carefully. And the proof would have to be found today. Bradley's frown, Bob's raised eyebrows and Julia's veiled insolence at afternoon tea had made it clear that their patience with her invasion of their property had been exhausted, and any attempt to repeat her visit would be resisted.

She reached the grove of trees and passed thankfully into its shadows. The Winns called it a "cattle camp"—the cattle sheltered there from heat and rain, and the air smelt strongly of them. The whole place was dim and strangely silent. Birdie stepped carefully through the trodden-down shrubs and piles of old manure, leaves and sticks rustling and crackling under her feet. She came to the edge closest to the road and looked carefully around her, pacing along the length of the grove, her eyes to the ground.

She soon found what she was looking for—a patch of flattened ground beside a tree stump, a cosy little hollow screened only by a few low, straggling bushes from the road winding through the valley floor, and the fields opposite. A couple of cigarette butts had been ground into the base of the stump, which had rotted and softened with age so as to make a comfortable back rest.

Birdie squatted on the ground next to the spot, and looked down the valley, across the road and over to the paddocks beyond. Then she slowly stood up and hesitated. She'd answered all her own questions. But now, for once, she didn't quite know what to do next. She stood and thought for a minute, then slowly turned and began to make her way through the sheltering trees and back up the hill.

They stood waiting for her, drawing together in the shadow of the verandah, silently watching. She grinned at them cheerfully and waved as she reached her car. She put her hand on the doorhandle, feeling its reassuring familiarity.

"Thanks for being so patient," she called. "I've finally finished. I'll get out of your hair now. Thanks again!"

In four strides Bradley Winn was down the verandah steps and facing her. "Oh, no," he growled. "No, you don't." He beckoned angrily.

"Bradley!" Julia's voice sounded cracked, and she cleared her throat.

Bradley stood his ground and beckoned to Birdie again. "You can just come and tell us what you've been up to round here. If you think you're going to piss off to town spreading rumours and lies about us just because you went to school with Marion Moore, you've got another think coming!"

"Take it easy, Brad." Bob Winn moved away from his wife and loomed up at the verandah rail. He frowned at Birdie. "We've given you the run of the place, haven't we?" he said coldly. "The least you can do, I'd say, is give us a chance to hear what you're going back to town with. Come up and have a drink." It was a demand, not an invitation.

Birdie patted her little car ruefully. Well, she hadn't really thought she'd get away with it. She pushed her glasses up on her nose and slowly moved towards the house. The Winns stood back as she climbed the stairs, and closed in behind her like guards as she walked through the old front door.

Again they sat around the big table, but this time Birdie sat at the head, and they waited for her to speak. Now that she had done what they had asked her to do, control seemed inexplicably to have passed into her hands again. Old Jean seemed faintly confused. She murmured something to Bob, who patted her hand awkwardly and shook his head.

"Are you sure you want me to go into this now?" asked Birdie, looking at him, and over to Bradley, glowering on the other side of the table in extraordinary contrast to Julia, who sat beside him elaborately at her ease, and faintly smiling.

"Why not?" he said coolly.

"You won't like it."

"That's not the point. Or maybe that is the point. If you've got the wrong end of the stick, I want to know about it before anyone else does. We all do."

She shrugged, and leaned forward on the table.

"I came here without any fixed ideas at all. Frankly, hearing the story at Marion's, and reading all the notes and newspaper reports she gave me, I could see why the cops had fixed on Davey Moore as the most likely person to have killed Bradley's wife. I told Marion that. But I came out here anyway, because I'd promised her I'd do what I could, and because I was curious.

"It became obvious pretty quickly that most of the people in this house had some sort of motive for killing Shirley Winn. Bob and Julia wanted to sell the farm and move into town, and Shirley was standing in their way through her influence over Bradley. Mrs. Jean Winn may have resented the power Shirley had over her, and the fact that Shirley had taken her place in the family. And Bradley himself seems to me to have been very ambivalent about his wife and the life she forced him to lead."

"You're mad!" Bradley stared at her venomously, spitting out the words.

"The problem for me was that the people with the most obvious motives had the most unshakeable alibis," Birdie went on, looking straight at Bob. "All of you were somewhere else, with witnesses to prove it, at the presumed time of the murder."

His grim mouth relaxed slightly. "We knew that before you arrived," he said. "Everyone knows that. Tell us something we don't know, will you?"

Birdie's eyes glittered behind her thick glasses. "Well, one thing you don't know, Mr. Winn, is that my experience has taught me to be extremely suspicious of cast-iron alibis. And I felt, after I'd been here a while, that given the tensions that had obviously existed between Shirley Winn and the rest of you, it was extremely convenient for you all that your various absences from this house at that particular time were so elaborately witnessed."

Julia shrugged, and her smile broadened. "You have to be lucky sometimes, honey!" she drawled.

Birdie nodded at her thoughtfully. "Yes, you do," she agreed quietly. "Anyway, aside from the alibis, there was something else that really puzzled me: why was the body hidden in the pumpkin vine? There seemed no rhyme or reason for it. Unless she was killed, not at the clothesline but very near where she was found, and rolled into the vine to hide the fact and time of her death from Mrs. Winn, who may at any time have looked out her bedroom window and seen the body."

"Well, that's probably exactly what Davey Moore did! There's no problem for us there," exclaimed Julia shrilly. "We were all gone before Jean went into bed, weren't we, Jean? And Shirley was fine when we left. Yelling at Davey when I left, hanging out the clothes when Bob and Bradley went. Isn't that right?"

The two men nodded, waiting.

"Did you see Shirley hanging out the clothes, Jean?" asked Birdie gently.

The old woman looked at her vacantly. "I . . . she was hanging out the clothes. I think I saw her," she mumbled. "Or maybe I just knew she was."

"Because someone told you?"

"Mum . . ." began Bob Winn warningly. But Jean Winn just stared at the tabletop, and said nothing.

"A conspiracy between you and Bradley, Bob, seemed to me not out of the question, under the circumstances," Birdie said calmly. "You could have killed Shirley as soon as Julia and Mrs. Winn were out of the way. You could have finished hanging out the clothes to fix the time of the murder as later than it was, then toddled off together to establish your alibis, couldn't you?"

"We . . ." Bob Winn had grown pale under his suntan, but his face remained stern and his voice level.

"I'm not going to listen to this!" Bradley, red and sweating, heaved himself to his feet. He towered over Birdie, his huge fists planted on the table before her, panting with anger.

"Sit down, Bradley!" Julia Winn had half-risen. She pulled at his arm, easing him back to his seat. "She's having you on. She knows it's not true, because—"

"Because," Birdie interrupted smoothly, "you couldn't possibly have hidden the body in the pumpkin vine without Davey Moore seeing you, could you? And Davey has said he saw you both leave before he did."

"You're a bit of a smart-alec, aren't you?" Bradley snarled. "Think it's funny to get at us, don't you? Well, you can bloody get out of here, that's what you can do. Before I kick you out. And you can tell Marion Moore from me that I'm sorry for her but that brother of hers is a menace, and the sooner he's locked up away from decent people the better I'll like it!"

"Davey Moore wouldn't hurt a fly," Jean Winn piped up hoarsely.

"Mum, you wouldn't know!" roared Bradley.

The old woman showed a flash of her former spirit. "I certainly would know, boy! I've known him all his life. Knew his poor mother, and his grandmother too. I'm telling you he's harmless as a baby."

"Well, Mum, whatever you say," murmured Bob Winn, "we've all just heard that our Sherlock Holmes here can't pin it on us. That leaves the theory of the wandering nut-case, and that leaves me as cold as it leaves the cops—or Davey Moore."

"There's always me," Julia put in archly.

"You're accounted for, Julia," said Bob sharply.

"Yes," said Birdie slowly. "You could hardly be reading down the paddock there, in front of witnesses, and also be up here killing Shirley, could you?"

"Guess not," agreed Julia brightly. "So . . ."

"Unless, of course, the witnesses, who after all were a good way away, were led astray, and took a red sunhat on a tree stump for a very still, reading lady." Birdie looked at the ceiling. "While the lady herself slipped up through the trees and up to the house without anyone seeing her at all. Bob, Bradley and Davey had gone by then. Jean was in her bedroom with the door shut. No one to see. No worries."

"You . . . that's . . ." Julia's painted mouth was opening and closing. She looked wide-eyed around the table, registering Jean's bewildered frown, Bradley's shock, Bob's disbelief and anger. "You can't go round wildly accusing people like this! What do you think you're doing?"

"I'm letting you know," said Birdie calmly, "that Davey Moore isn't going to go down without a fight. I'd rather have a confession, but if I have to I'll make sure he's not the only one with a circumstantial case to answer. I know how Shirley Winn was killed, and when. I know why her body was found where it was. I know who killed her, and I think I know why. Do you understand?" She looked slowly round the table, her glasses shining in the yellow light of the lamp that swung above their heads.

Julia drew a sharp breath. "Clever, aren't you!" she hissed. "All right then, Miss Clever. Tell us! Tell us!"

Birdie smiled grimly. "It'd be better if you heard about it first-hand, don't you think?" Her eyes slid to the left. "All right, Jean, how about it?" she said gently. "Are you ready now, to tell them how you did it? Or will I?"

Jean Winn stared straight ahead. Her lips hardly moved as she began speaking.

"In town, in hospital, you know—it's not so bad. It's cool there. It's comfy. I had the TV in my room there. Silly little bits of nurses, pretty little things, some of them, in and out all day. Makes a change." She sighed, a deep, soft sigh. "Julia knows. She was keen for me to stay. But Shirley said no. Shirley got me out, and brought me back to this place, and Shirley said she'd make sure I never had to leave it again. She said I wouldn't leave this place till I died. She said I'd leave it over her dead body. Well . . ."

"Mum! Mum, what are you saying?" Bradley frantically reached out to the wrinkled hand, and for the first time his mother looked at him.

"She had you beat, didn't she, boy?" she said, smiling slightly, patting the hand that held hers and then pushing it gently away. "Just like me with your father. I could see it. I didn't like it.

"That afternoon, it was hot. This house, it's always been a hot house. And the dust. No matter what you do, the dust comes up through those floorboards. It's no good anymore. No comfort in it. Not when you're old and sick like me. And I went into bed and I could hear her voice, yelling at you, and poor, simple Davey Moore, and Julia had got fed up and left, and Bob couldn't do anything, and I thought . . . Julia won't stick this, I thought. She'll go. And Bob'll follow her. And I'll be here with her, and Bradley, and I'll never get out."

In the paddock, a cow bellowed, and another murmured in answer. The shadows on the paddock were long and the road a dusty grey strip in the valley floor. Inside the house the people sat motionless, gripping the table like people adrift at sea, holding on to a piece of flotsam, while around them the house sank into darkness.

The cracked voice droned on. "Davey went back outside. I heard her say she was going out to the line, even though she knew I was waiting for her to come. At the hospital they don't keep you waiting like that. Everything happens like clockwork there. The boys left. I heard them go. It was hot. I knelt up on the bed, to try and get the window open, but I couldn't budge it. It's like me and everything in this place. Old, and useless. It was so hot. I saw Davey Moore down tools and leave. I thought, good! Let the cattle in. I hate cabbage. I hate pumpkin. I always have.

"She came in. She ticked me off for kneeling up, like I was a kid. She got up beside me and pushed up the window, and she'd just stuck in one chock when she saw Davey heading off, and the fence still down. Way away by then, he was, but she couldn't leave it. Oh, no. She leant right over that bedhead and stuck her scrawny neck out that window and started yelling at him to come back. He couldn't hear her, but she didn't care. She just yelled, with the veins sticking out of her neck and her skirt all bunched up round her legs and her dirty shoes all over my clean cover, and I put up my hand and pulled out the chock and I thought, right, and I shoved that window down—right down on that skinny little neck." Jean looked, almost in wonder, at her blue-veined hand. "Killed her right off," she said calmly. "Never made a sound. Just fell forward, half out my window, half in. I didn't want her there. I got underneath her with my head and shoulders and pulled up on the bedhead and out she went. Out she went. Out of my house. Out. Then I lay down and had my rest. It was hot, but I got off all right. Woke up with a headache, though. Still . . ."

The clock struck in the heavy silence.

"The body rolled down the hill," said Birdie quietly. "Rolled down, and into the pumpkin vine. Then, after a while, the cattle came through the hole in the fence and wandered around, covering up all the traces of what had really happened."

She looked at the stricken faces around the table. "Sorry," she said. "You should've let me go. It's awful for you to hear it like this."

"Mum . . ." Bob Winn began, but his mother wasn't listening to him. She was smiling to herself.

"Woke up with a shocking headache," she nodded. "But it was worth it."

"Birdie, we can't thank you enough." Marion Moore sat on the end of the guestroom bed, beaming at her friend. "I knew you'd do it. I never doubted it for a minute."

She didn't, either, Birdie realised. It must be great, sometimes, to have such an unswerving faith in happy endings. When everything worked out. "That's okay, Marion," she said, and suddenly yawned. "Oh, sorry. God, I'm tired."

"Country air!" smiled Marion. "It's good for you. I'll let you get off to sleep. But listen, you've never said what put you onto Jean. I mean, how you worked out who did it."

Birdie sank back into her pillows. "Well, I didn't really work out who did it at all, Marion. I worked out who didn't do it. Bob couldn't have and Bradley couldn't have, because Davey would have seen them stash the body. Julia couldn't have, because she was in clear view of the boys across the way all the time. I was sure she wasn't the one, but I did do a final check just to see if she could have pulled a swifty. There were only two straggly little bushes, though, between the spot where she was sitting and the road. No one would have been fooled by a stump with a hat on it for a minute at the distance. But I'd already decided by then that old Jean was the only real possibility. See, Shirley's hat was on its peg in the living room. They told me Shirley always wore her hat outside. Yet there it was inside, untouched, Julia told me, since her death. She'd come in, hung up her hat, and been killed inside the house." She yawned again, and Marion stood up, but remained hovering hopefully by the door.

"Then when I saw Jean's room," Birdie continued wearily, "I realised how the murder could have been done, and how the body could have ended up in the pumpkin patch. Simple, really. All I had to do was get her to confess. She's very frail, Marion. She'll never make it to trial, you know. She'll end her days in the nice, cool hospital just like she wanted. But at least Davey's safe now. So you got what you wanted, too."

"You're very clever, Birdie." Marion nodded seriously from the doorway. She hesitated, bit her lip and rushed on. "But listen, dear, how did you decide that—that Davey wasn't the guilty one? I mean, he could have gone into the house and done it, couldn't he? He could have hidden the body in the vine just because he was scared. How did you know he was innocent?"

Birdie stared at her for a minute, then she took off her glasses, laid them on the bedside table, and closed her eyes.

"I seem to have taken that on trust, Marion," she said, almost in wonder. "I think I'd better leave quite early tomorrow morning. Whatever you've got must be catching. I wouldn't want it to get a grip on me. It'd be the end of a brilliant career."

Marion Moore smiled. "Sweet dreams," she murmured. And turned off the light.

DEATH
WARMED UP

ON THE DAY THE MOST unpleasant woman in Bangalow Beach was to die, the morning began like any other.

It was early, just after ten, but already the beach was filling up. The promise of heat buzzed in the air, and methodically the people set up camp on the sand, arranging towels, umbrellas, bags of food and drink—staking out their boundaries, politely averting their eyes from neighbouring encampments. Then, safely anonymous behind their sunglasses, they peeled themselves down to tender seminudity and lay back, oiled and creamed, to bake.

"It's bizarre," said Verity Birdwood, hunched fully clothed on one end of her friend Kate's striped beach towel. "Look at them, will you? And look at you! Do you know the skin cancer statistics in Australia, Kate?"

"Birdie, just relax, will you? That's what we're here for."

"That's what you're here for. I don't know why I'm here. I hate the beach."

"You hate everything that's good for you." Kate sighed contentedly as the sun warmed her back. She dug her toes into the dry sand, to feel the cool, damp layers below.

"Good for you! Sunburn, jellyfish, sharks—people!" muttered Birdie sourly. She glowered at a party of three squeaking its way across the sand. The newcomers appeared not to notice and began settling down beside her.

"Do we have to huddle in with the mob, Doug? Honestly!" The high, spoilt voice cut through the drowsy air. A few people nearby lifted their heads to look.

The small, blond woman with a deep suntan and enormous white-framed sunglasses was in her mid-forties, by the look of her, Birdie thought, but her figure was almost that of a young girl. Her voice though, that was something else. Affected, brittle and carrying, it almost set one's teeth on edge. Birdie watched her and noted that the tall dark man setting up the beach umbrella simply shrugged his massive shoulders a little and continued with his task.

"I can't face that way, Doug. My head's too bad. Oh, God! Andy! Help him, will you!" The woman put her hand to her forehead, as one who is being sorely tried.

The gangling boy hovering behind her with a large bag moved forward, blushing. He was a slightly-built young man with a weak, sensitive mouth and fine, fair hair that flopped limply over his forehead. He, at least, was all too aware of the lazily amused glances being directed at them.

The woman settled herself on a towel spread for her, removed her skirt to reveal a white swimsuit, and shook her bracelets back to her elbows.

"Put down the bag and sit, Andy," she commanded, patting the towel and smiling at him briefly.

He muttered something and glanced over his shoulder.

"What? Well, what's she doing here?" The woman lifted her

sunglasses and gazed haughtily across the sand. A girl in a black bikini waved and nodded in her direction. The woman replaced her sunglasses and, without a sign of recognition, turned and lay down on her stomach. It was a very deliberate snub.

"Honestly, Andy!" Her voice carried, even from that position. "If you must dabble with little dolly birds, please be discreet about it and keep them away from me!"

The boy stared at her blindly for a moment, then turned and stumbled away.

"Young idiot!" exclaimed the woman.

"Marjorie, you're the idiot. Why set up this meeting if all you're going to do is nag him?" murmured the dark man, squatting beside her. "He's moved out of your house as it is. D'you want him out of your life as well?"

The woman thinned her lips. "He's just a boy. He needs direction. Deidre Hewitt is a common little gold digger. She's fooled poor Andy, but not me. And she knows it." She closed her eyes. "He'll be back. She'll make sure of that. She doesn't want Andy cut off without a cent. Let's face it, he isn't much of a catch without a loaded, doting stepmother, is he?"

The man turned his heavy head away from her. "You're a bitch, you know that, Marjorie?" he said quietly. "That's Andy's father's money you're talking about."

"It's my money now, Doug." The woman's voice was hard. "Andy's daddy's deadibones. The grieving widow's married to you now, sweetie. The money's in my name. I can leave it to whom I choose. At the moment, that's Andy, with you as understudy. But Andy'd better learn which side his bread's buttered on, or . . ." She yawned. "Get me a drink, darling. I feel frightful. Coke and a little something stronger."

"Marjorie, you only had breakfast half an hour ago. Give it a rest. You're killing yourself with that stuff." The man stood up and stripped off his shirt. "I'm going to the headland to meet Jock," he said. "Andy's got the bag. Talk to him about it. But if you take my advice, you'll leave the booze alone for once."

The woman writhed into a sitting position and glared at him. "Drop dead!" she hissed.

"Be back at lunchtime." He walked away from her without looking back. At the waterline he turned and began to jog slowly down the beach.

"Andy! Andy! Here!" Marjorie was red with anger. She beckoned imperiously at her stepson, sitting in deep conversation with the girl in the black bikini. The boy rose and reluctantly obeyed the summons.

"Don't sulk, Andy." The woman forced a smile. "Be a good boy and get me a drink. Coke and the doings, you know how I like it. You have the bag, you know."

"Okay." The boy shifted from foot to foot. "Marjorie, I wish you'd . . . you'll have to accept that I'm going to get engaged to Deidre, and—"

Marjorie threw back her head and screeched with laughter. "Oh Andy, you're priceless sometimes. Engaged! Oh dear, dear, you proper old thing." She looked at him, her face distorted with mirth. An ugly red flush rose on his cheeks.

"It's not funny. I've talked to Doug about it, and he thought if you and I and Deidre could just—"

Her face closed with a snap.

"Leave Doug out of this, if you don't mind. It's no business of his, and his opinion doesn't matter a cracker. This is between you and me, Andy, and I'm telling you, if you get tied up with that second-rate little tart you can kiss any help from me good-bye. And any hope of the boodle after I'm gone, for that matter. That's a promise, Andy!"

He stared at her, white-faced. His hands were shaking. "It's my money, Marjorie. Dad meant you to—"

"It is in no sense your money. It's my money. To do with as I like, when I like. You understand me? Now for God's sake bring me that drink!"

Birdie saw the boy stumble back to his ladylove, vanquished. The sand was warm under her feet. The water crashed and rushed up the shore, hissing and bubbling. After a few moments she watched, fascinated, as Andy trudged by and delivered Marjorie's bag, and her drink. Apparently it hadn't occurred to him to let her whistle for it. Extraordinary.

"It's marvellous in, Birdie. You don't know what you're missing!" Kate flopped onto her towel and turned her face to the sun, now high in the sky.

Birdie shrugged. "Cold and wet and hair full of sand, that's what I'm missing," she said loftily. She glanced to where the bronzed Marjorie lay spreadeagled under the beach umbrella, Coca-Cola can at her hand. "Not everyone has your need for vigorous physical effort, Kate. Some of us have other interests."

"Snooping, for instance," hissed Kate.

"It's interesting."

"I can't see what's so interesting about a nasty, tiddly woman sleeping it off. Even her family are giving her a wide berth. Anyway," Kate glanced at the sky, "it's going to cloud over soon, and I'm getting hungry. What time is it?"

"Twelve-thirty."

"We'll go back to the house soon, eh? Put you out of your misery?"

"I'm okay. Whenever you like."

Birdie sat primly on the sand, the only clothed and upright soul among a hundred. Everywhere people lay silent, gleaming, motionless—on their backs, like Kate, or on their stomachs, like the unpleasant Marjorie. Farther along the beach, near the rock pools and the car park, family groups shouted and played. In the water at the other headland surfboard riders floated, waiting for the next wave, and a few fishermen risked their lives one more time on the slippery rock shelves. But here, on this stretch of sand, it was as though a massacre had occurred. Every now and then, rather disconcertingly, one of the bodies would heave, sit up, reapply oil and lie down again to roast the other side. A shame, Birdie thought, they couldn't arrange to be turned automatically, like chickens on a spit.

The sun dimmed, and the people stirred. First one, then another, sat up, but didn't make the automatic turn. Instead they glanced at the sky, dug in a bag for a watch, sighed, and began to pack up their belongings. The young Andy and his black-bikinied amour unlinked their hands and stood up. They turned to glance in the still-recumbent Marjorie's direction and murmured together. Surely they weren't going to risk another encounter? The boy stood and squinted towards the headland. He raised his arm in a self-conscious greeting.

Birdie saw that the indefatigable Doug was on his way back, jogging along the waterline. "Looks like Tarzan of the apes," she muttered.

"What?" Kate stirred and sat up. She looked at the sky and at Birdie's watch, sighed and started packing up her belongings.

"That guy. Princess Charming's husband. He looks like someone out of an old movie. Huge chest, tiny little skintight shorts . . ."

"Yeah. Dazzling, isn't he?"

"Well, I don't know about dazzling. Prehistoric was more the word I was after."

"The lovely Marjorie probably appreciates him. Strong, silent type. Opposites attract, you know."

"Kate, your freshness of language always takes my breath away!"

Kate yawned unconcernedly. "It's the truth, nonetheless," she said. "God, she can relax all right, anyway. She's been lying like that for hours. No wonder she's so brown."

Birdie frowned. Now the beach was clearing rapidly. A rather unpleasant breeze had sprung up, flapping umbrellas and scattering flimsy belongings.

The big man dropped gradually from a jog to a walk. He strode up the sand towards them. He reached his wife, and for a moment stood above her still form, his brow furrowed. Then he bent and rummaged in the bag at her feet. He pulled out a small flask of whisky. It was still three-quarters full. He tossed it back, rummaged again and then appeared to lose heart. He straightened up and nudged his wife none too gently with a bare foot. Marjorie didn't stir. He grimaced and knelt beside her, his fists clenched. "Marjorie," he murmured, glancing quickly towards Birdie and Kate, the last potential eavesdroppers nearby. "Come on. Time to go."

There was no movement. He ducked his heavy head in frustration. "Look, not again. I can't stand this, Marjorie! Snap out of it!" His tight fists were eloquent. Kate looked away in embarrassment, grabbed her bag and stood up. She wasn't going to snoop anymore. Birdie could do what she liked.

"Andy!"

Kate spun around in shock. The man had yelled at the top of his voice. He had sprung to his feet and was backing away from the woman lying so still on the sand.

The boy ran up to him, eyes startled and enquiring.

"Get help," said Doug, Tarzan no longer, just a heavy worried man. "Marjorie's . . ."

"She only had one drink, Doug. I only gave her one. It was strong, but just one couldn't . . ."

"She's not bloody drunk, Andy. I think she's dead."

"What?" The girl in the black bikini, Deidre the despised,

was behind them, grabbing at the boy's hand. Her heavily made-up eyes blinked rapidly, her mouth hung a little open.

"Don't look, Deidre." Andy made a rather pathetic attempt to shield her with his thin body. She buried her face in his bony shoulder and burst into loud sobs.

Doug looked at them helplessly. Birdie saw that his big fists were clenched so tightly that the knuckles showed white. She stood up and walked over to him. "Can I help?" she said. He just stared at her. She knelt by the small, still body for a moment and felt for a pulse. The flesh she touched was cooling fast.

Birdie put down her coffee cup and smiled at Douglas Freeman gratefully. Kate would have been surprised to see how frail and tentative she looked at this moment. "You're very kind, all of you, to have brought me back with you like this." She glanced at Andy and Deidre, sitting together like two limp and slightly scruffy tourists, amid the potted palms on Marjorie's verandah, with its extraordinary view and its swimming pool below.

"No worries," said Doug. "Least I could do. The cops were pretty thorough, weren't they?" He was pale and tired himself, but at least now he had relaxed. His hands hung loose in his lap, he leaned back in his chair.

"They don't think it's suicide, you know," he said, without looking at her. "They think it's murder. And I'm suspect number one. The husband always is. God knows, Marjorie wasn't an easy woman to live with—anyone could see that."

"No one would suspect you, Doug," said Deidre, opening her eyes wide and leaning forward. "You put up with such a lot. We told them that. It's not as if you have anything to gain, anyway. Andy gets the house and the money and everything now."

"Shut up, Deidre!" Andy's voice sounded strangled. Deidre glanced at him sharply, but decided not to argue. He'd been drinking wine steadily since arriving at the house and was having trouble keeping his eyes open.

"They said the dregs in the Coke can were full of white powder," said Doug, ignoring them both. "Sleeping pills, her sort they think. Sleeping pills and whisky. Enough to kill a horse." He shut his eyes.

Birdie stretched. "They haven't got much to test. It's a shame the can got knocked over."

"I couldn't help it!" snapped Deidre defensively. "And Doug got to it in time, didn't he? There was some left."

"I don't know why I bloody did rush for it, now," grumbled Doug. "Just instinct. Stupid. Now they think it's murder. And I'm in the gun."

"No, you're not," said Birdie quietly.

He stared at her.

"Think it out," she said patiently. "You weren't even there when the drink was poured and drunk, were you?"

"No, but . . ." He sighed and shook his head. "God knows, I felt like killing her, often enough. Terrible thing to say, but it's true. It would've been easy, alone here like we were. A quick flick over the balcony, a hand on the head in the pool, so easy. And now . . ."

"Don't go on about it!" Andy struggled upright, blinking at them with glazed eyes. "Some lunatic did it, that's what probably happened. For fun."

"I think that's pretty unlikely," said Birdie gently.

"You're saying that Doug or Andy did it, then, are you?" shrilled Deidre, suddenly aggressive. "That's just ridiculous."

"Well, as the police would see it," said Birdie patiently, "there were obvious motives for both of them, and, in Andy's case at least, opportunity. Andy gave her a drink. And in that drink traces of a drug were found." She looked around calmly. "And no one else went near her from that point on. I was sitting next to her. I heard and saw everything from the moment she arrived on the beach."

"Awfully observant, aren't you?" sneered Deidre, jumping up. "I would've thought even someone like you would have better things to do on the beach than stick your nose into other people's business!" She flounced angrily off into the house.

Birdie smiled; the men looked embarrassed.

"What was the story on the bloody drink, anyhow, Andy?" muttered Doug.

The boy flicked his head back impatiently. "Oh, you know, the usual thing. Deidre opened the Coke and tipped some of it out, while I looked for the Scotch in that bloody huge bag of Marjorie's. I finally found it and put some in the can. The whisky was fine, a new bottle."

"Andy," said Doug slowly, "mate, you didn't tell the cops Deidre opened the Coke?"

"What does it matter?"

"Everything matters, Andy," said Birdie. "You should tell them."

Andy stared at her blankly. "What do you mean?" he mumbled, struggling to focus.

"Don't worry about it now, mate," said Doug hastily. "Just relax, okay?"

Andy looked at them sulkily for a moment, then lay back in his chair and closed his eyes.

"He's tired," murmured Doug apologetically. "God, I'm tired too. The cops made me go over every detail of this morning. Was she depressed? Manic, I'd call it. Any other day it's lie in till the last minute, coffee in bed at nine-thirty or ten, dawdle around. Today it was coffee at seven, walk, swim in the pool, then off to the beach. I couldn't understand it, but now I think she was looking forward to seeing Andy. I'd organised the meeting. It's been a while. It's ironic," he said. "Poor kid."

Birdie rose. "I think I'd better go now," she said, not meeting his eye.

"Sure, I'll drive you. No, I insist. It's the least I can do. You're the witness who's saving my bacon, aren't you? Stand where you are and drink in the view. I'll go and get the keys."

Birdie stood by the verandah rail. The clouds had blown away now, and late afternoon sunshine flooded the scene before her.

The house was built on a steep slope. Two floors down, the pool sparkled turquoise in a grove of tree ferns. Below that again, waves crashed against a small rocky beach. As she looked down, her stomach turned over in a shudder of vertigo.

Suddenly she had the feeling that she was being watched. Slowly she turned, but there was nothing to be seen. Only the curtains moving softly in the breeze, and Andy slumped in his chair, eyes closed.

She turned back to the rail, but the back of her neck was prickling. She waited. Prepared as she was, the soft rush of footsteps behind her came faster, far faster than she'd dreamed, and the hands that grabbed for her mouth and waist were like snakes, hauling and pulling her off balance, tipping her against and over the rails towards that terrible drop. No planned action saved her, only an instinctive twist that put her attacker off balance enough for her to slip free, to run—across the verandah, away from that dizzying height, through the living room and up the stairs to the front door, with thudding footfalls behind her, catching up, and a hundred steep steps between her and the public road.

She reached the door, pulled it open—and only then did she scream, darting between the two big men who stood, astonished, on the doorstep. She fell, shaking, against the mossy steps, heard the yell of frustration and rage her attacker gave, heard the struggle begin.

The police were big burly men. But it took both of them, and a pair of handcuffs, to finally subdue Doug Freeman, and take him away.

Birdie sat with Kate, drinking tea.

"I'd started thinking that Doug Freeman must have killed his wife," she said, "because he was the only one of the three of them who needed her to die in a public place. As he himself pointed out, rather forcefully, there were plenty of opportunities to dispose of her at home. But then, you see, he'd be the natural, indeed the only, suspect. And even if he got away with it, he wouldn't get any money. He had to frame Andy, her heir, to have any chance at that. But I just couldn't see how he could've got to that can of Coke. That was the stumbling block."

Kate looked at her friend with mingled affection and concern. Birdie's freckled face was pale, and her left arm was bandaged.

"But how did he know you thought that, Birdie? What made him go for you like that?"

"He made a slip, and I saw it. I heard him say to Marjorie, at ten-fifteen, when she asked him for a drink, that she'd only had breakfast "half an hour ago"—that meant nine-thirty or quarter to ten. But repeating to me what he told the cops, he emphasised that she'd breakfasted very early, at seven. And then I remembered what he'd said at the beach, and realised why he was lying. And he saw it. The Coke can was a complete red herring. He poisoned Marjorie at home, in her morning coffee, at nine-thirty or nine forty-five, then he took her to the beach, arranged it so Andy would get her a drink, which she always demanded, and left her there to die. Just one sprawled-out body among many."

"But the Coke was drugged."

"Of course. He put the stuff in after the event. While we were waiting for the cops. There were plenty of opportunities then. No wonder he rushed to save the can when Deidre knocked it over. The last thing he wanted was for the evidence against Andy to disappear."

Kate shook her head. "Quite clever. Not as prehistoric as you thought, was he, Birdie?" Then she sat up. "But where did he hide all those pills? He was practically stark naked. No pockets—no place to hide the smallest thing!" She almost blushed.

Birdie grinned. "Simple. He rummaged in her bag, just before he pretended to try and wake her, as though he was looking to see how much whisky she'd drunk. But he must have had the pills stashed somewhere. He just took them loose in his hand and kept his fist clenched all the time. I thought it was tension—felt quite sorry for him, heaven forbid. When he grabbed me later at the house his hands still reeked of that medicine smell. He must have held onto those pills for ages."

"Unpleasant characters," said Kate thoughtfully, "he and his wife?"

"Yes." Birdie grinned. "Like attracted to like, Kate? As opposed to opposites attracting? The exception that proves the rule, perhaps? But all's well that ends well! You'd say that, wouldn't you, Kate?"

"You're pathetic, Birdie!"

Birdie sniggered. "And you're sunburnt," she said.

FLASHPOINT

WHEN JEREMY HEARD ABOUT the death he started to wish he'd listened more closely to his wife's conversation over the last few days. But with the STD calls racking up dollars—his employer's dollars, to be sure, but dollars nevertheless—he hadn't wanted to waste time with gossip about what the appalling Claudia Budd had said about Juliette Nimmo and her doings. He wanted even less to hear about Kate's friend Verity Birdwood's attitude to the whole thing. He'd just wanted to make sure all was well and then get down to important things like how tired he was, how hot it had been, and what a bastard of a job this was, and receiving a moderately large dose of Kate's sympathy and interest.

The cab driver taking him home from the airport knew only the barest details. But Kate would be sure to know a lot more. Claudia had been living in the house for the last week, having leapt at the opportunity provided by Jeremy's absence to leave Wally, her own long-suffering partner, to stew in his own juice, as she put it, and realise how bereft he'd be without her. Kate was full of sympathy for Claudia's situation, and delighted at the prospect of having her company for the week. Claudia was news editor for one of the weekly women's magazines. Hyperactive, slim as a whip, painted and bedizened beyond all normal bounds of sense or taste, cynical beyond belief, Claudia trailed glitz, gossip and hilarity in her wake and Kate found her riveting company. Jeremy felt differently, and his immediate fear on hearing of her visit was that Wally, instead of seeing the error of his ways, would realise how wonderful life could be without Claudia, and refuse to have her back, leaving her to occupy their spare room until a new love interest came along. Which, at Claudia's age, could be quite a while.

In fact Jeremy felt quite tense as the cab drew up at his front door, and absurdly relieved to find Kate waiting for him alone. The house was cool and quiet, their daughter Zoe peacefully asleep upstairs. The only signs of Claudia's recent presence were a huge vase of bizarrely bright gladioli in a corner of the living room, some empty bottles of Moët in the kitchen, and the smell of her musky perfume, which seemed to have penetrated every cushion, curtain and corner.

"When did Claudia go, then?" he asked casually, after they'd settled with a cup of tea in the kitchen.

"This morning. She knew you were coming back tonight. I said she could stay, but she wouldn't. She doesn't think you approve of her," said Kate, with a note of reproach.

"I wonder why she'd think that? Did she go back to poor Wally?"

"I don't know why you say 'poor,' Jeremy. You've got no idea what she puts up with from that man. Anyway, yes, she did go back. So."

"Bet she loved the death. Rushing round stopping the presses, was she? Organising interviews with the nearest and dearest? Digging out file pictures she could caption 'In happier days'? Oh, she has a full life, our Claudia."

Kate looked down her nose at him. "You needn't sneer, Jeremy. Claudia's very good at what she does. Even Birdie sees that. She talked about her just like you do at first, but you know what happened today?"

"I have no idea and care not a fig! Next to Claudia, Verity Birdwood is the person whose doings interest me the least."

"Birdie called in here a few times while Claudia was staying and gradually she got interested," said Kate loftily. "Birdie, at least, can see beyond her nose and her prejudices where people are concerned."

"I see. Well, what did the perspicacious Birdwood think of the suicide? She's always interested in a good death, isn't she? Nice for her and Claudia to have something in common. I can see my being away has been a blessing in disguise. All these cosy girls-together chats. Glamour and death fourth-hand. Lovely for you."

Kate smiled sweetly. "You've been in the sticks too long," she said sympathetically. "Sad how it blunts one's instincts. You've got no idea what's been going on here in your absence. High drama, passion and betrayal . . . the mystery unfolds . . ."

"What is that supposed to mean?"

"I'll tell you, when you've finished knocking my friends."

"All right, I've finished. Tell."

"From the beginning, or it won't make sense. Okay?"

"All right, all right. Just get on with it."

"Well," Kate began, "you can imagine how hyped-up Claudia's been about Juliette Nimmo's visit—the thrill of the chase, you know?"

"It's ridiculous! That bimbo—"

"People are interested, Jeremy. It's the classic local girl

makes good. Two sensational movies and coming home to promote a third with a huge star like Paul Frere in tow."

"I thought she was on with the co-star."

"Claudia says that's PR hype for the movie. Halkyn Spiers and Juliette knew each other here years ago, and they say he's been carrying a torch for her, but everyone knows she's really on with Paul Frere."

"He must be twenty-five years older than her. Old letch. He just goes from one little girl to another."

"Yeah, well they've been hanging around together for over a year. Ever since they did *Final Sonata* together. Claudia says they're besotted. And why else would he be out here with her? He's not in *Flashpoint*. But they keep up the 'just good friends' line. No one's ever got them to say anything different."

"She was hanging all over him at the airport. I saw the great arrival. They do have TV in Kalgoorlie, you know. I thought she looked awful."

"Claudia says she's exhausted. Jaded. And very aggro. Had her nose and teeth done, Claudia says, since she left, and a personality makeover as well. Claudia says she used to be very fresh and sweet. She interviewed her lots of times for *Hers* before she went away. But since she's had the star treatment the inevitable's happened. This time Claudia couldn't get anything exclusive at all. So of course she was spitting chips, and packing it in case Juliette's publicity guy was spinning her a line and had actually given an exclusive to the enemy—you know, *She.*

"Anyhow, apparently he wasn't. Having her on, I mean. Juliette was here for the premiere of *Flashpoint,* and before the official bits and pieces for that she was going to have a fortnight's holiday, with no interviews or anything formal at all. She said she just wanted to spend some time with her family, especially her little sister Alexandra whom she'd missed *so* much, and her darling dad. And she wanted to show Paul her *beautiful* country, which, did we realise, was *so* like America was twenty years ago. Everyone in LA said so. She just wanted to rest. She needed to be alone." Kate rolled her eyes and Jeremy smiled. He felt peaceful and rather drowsy, hunched over his cup at the kitchen table. Kalgoorlie seemed a million miles away. Well, it was, practically. He poured more tea.

"So of course *Hers* and *She* understood and respected that," he said drily, "and they published the airport and press conference photographs and some stills from *Flashpoint* in their next edition, and left the loving couple in peace for the fortnight. Or could I be wrong?"

"You could. They pursued Juliette and Paul like . . . well, every press photographer in Sydney was after them, apparently. Not just the magazines. They were staying at the Imperial and tried to slip in and out, but Claudia, for one, had people watching the place day and night, and she'd told all the freelancers she'd pay big money for pictures. Especially ones the other lot didn't get. But her photographers kept bumping into *She* photographers all the time, because they were all trailing the lovebirds round the city and in and out of parks and all that.

"Everywhere they went, a herd of press went too. 'If she wants to be quiet,' I said to Claudia, 'why on earth stay at the Imperial? Why not sneak into Australia as Mr. and Mrs. Smith and go quietly to stay somewhere private?'

"Birdie was here then. She'd been sitting there looking bored and above it all but when I said that, she smiled in this smug way and said, 'Well, obviously no one would act like Juliette Nimmo unless they *wanted* to be photographed and chased around.' She said the whole thing was plainly a PR stunt and the press was being manipulated. As usual.

"So Claudia, who'd sized Birdie up earlier and got her wrong, like people do, did a little double-take, then recovered, smiled very sweetly back and said, as though she was speaking to quite a young child, that everyone knew very well what they were about.

" 'It's a game we play, sweetie,' she said to Birdie. 'She's using us, we're using her, and everyone gets what they want.' You should have seen Birdie's face! Claudia screamed laughing. 'Oh, I know. Tacky, tacky, sweetie, but there you are! It's a game—but if you want to know, this time I think my team won!'

"Birdie just went on looking sour. Claudia had had quite a bit of champagne by then, and she was terribly vibed-up anyhow. She grabbed Birdie's arm. 'I shouldn't show you this,' she said, 'but it'll be out tomorrow, won't it, so what the hell? And I'm so happy!' She shoved her other hand into her bag and pulled out a magazine and slapped it down on the coffee table. 'How's *that!*' she yelled out, like an overexcited bowler at a Test match. She was positively beaming, and she looked at Birdie and me as if she was expecting us to start frothing at the mouth or something.

"Well, you know those *Hers* covers. They all look the same to me, and they're a bit hard to focus on—there's so much going on. But anyway there was this fuzzy-looking photo bang in the middle. Two people beside a swimming pool in a very tight clinch, the woman only wearing a bikini bottom, or maybe even panties. And this huge slash of type right across saying 'Juliette and Paul—their torrid love—Scoop! Pics!'

"Birdie actually took off her glasses and rubbed at her eyes as if she was in pain. Claudia was jiggling up and down, grinning all over her face. 'It'll sell its *tits* off!' she shouted. She woke Zoe up, actually, she was so loud.

"Inside the magazine there were more photos. A lot of them were fuzzy too, but they were all very tame and decorous. Juliette with darling dad and sister at airport, face very close to sis's so you could see that though they looked alike, Juliette had the star quality; Juliette and Paul 'mingling with the crowd like any happy holidaymakers' at the Quay; Juliette and Paul in the park; Juliette and Paul ducking into the back of a stretch limo; Juliette and Paul buying fruit at a market. Fully dressed and discreet, hardly touching, 'in disguise' in jeans and T-shirts, hats and sunglasses, bounding along in sensible running shoes and obviously completely aware they were being watched.

" 'So they won that round,' Claudia said. 'And everyone had the same thing, and I was so depressed! Frank Nimmo, the dad, wouldn't talk. He's a conservative old bastard, and I was hoping he'd rip into Paul Frere or something for me. But no go. And Alexandra Nimmo, who's a nice girl, finally got sick of being asked how it felt to have a fabulous star for a sister and went underground. I had nothing! And then, at the absolute last second . . .' She turned back to the front cover and stroked the fuzzy swimming pool picture like you'd pat a baby's head. So gently and lovingly. 'We were just about to go to print on the cover when this turned up. I couldn't believe it! And no one else's got this. No one's *ever* had anything like this. That mad bitch Christian Flower got herself into the hotel with a camera in a shoulder bag, stayed up all night ducking security and prowling around, never saw hide nor hair of them, gave up, went up to the pool to wake herself up and by this absolute fluke there they were having a swim! At five in the morning! You wouldn't believe the luck! She shot the whole series through a wicker screen beside the changing room. They had no idea. What a pro! Oh, *She* will be livid!'

"Birdie said she supposed Juliette would be pretty livid too. Claudia said Juliette was a pro herself and understood the rules. I was thinking I wouldn't much like that sort of picture being splashed all over the front cover of a national magazine, however much of a pro I was. The inside ones were absolutely different. You know the sort of thing—'just friends,' as they say. 'Just good friends,' and very sweet and natural, and a lovely couple. He so big, with the white-blond hair, so tall, so strong, so famous, so rich. And her so young, so fragile beside him, her black curly head reaching just to his cleft chin, and so unspoiled, so beautiful, so high-profile . . ."

"Kate, you've spent too much time with Claudia," Jeremy said. "You're getting as cynical as she is."

"No one could be as cynical as Claudia and live! Except Birdie. She looked at the cover picture carefully and then looked at Claudia through those thick glasses of hers like a little owl, and said in this mild little voice, 'It's very intense, isn't it? If they feel like that about each other, if they've been lovers for a year, isn't it odd that they could be so restrained in public? You'd think it would show through a bit, wouldn't you?' She turned to the inside pictures and pored over them. It was funny seeing Birdie so interested in something she'd usually consider *so* tacky.

"But Claudia didn't think it was funny. This had been life and death to her for a fortnight, after all, and she nodded seriously and said that it seemed odd to us but after all they were actors. While the press was watching, they played a part, she said. But when they were alone, or thought they were alone . . . it was different. They'd been particularly difficult this trip. They'd only really started to relax this week—too late for this issue—and anyway, only to the extent that they'd sometimes been photographed in America. She pointed at the set of pictures taken at the market. 'This was the last set we took before deadline on this issue,' she said. 'They'd been here about five days then. I was going to have to use one of these on the cover. You see, he's looking at her a bit more intensely there, and his hand could be on her waist. You can't see because of her jacket, and the pic's small here, but . . .'

"Birdie and I squinted at the little image on the page. I couldn't see any particularly intense look myself, and his hand could have been anywhere. Claudia was grasping at straws there, I thought.

"Birdie shrugged. 'Maybe,' she said. 'But I can't see the reason for them being so circumspect. I mean, why the big act? And why more here than America?'

"Claudia got superior again. 'Her image is squeaky clean, not sexy,' she said patiently. 'She's fresh and unspoiled, remember? Which is the biggest laugh these days, but however. And she's at home. And she's got her family to consider. Her father really is very straight-laced. And Paul Frere has a terrible reputation as a womaniser. They have to be careful. Besides, the PR people are madly trying to create a love triangle with Juliette, Paul and Halkyn Spiers, for the movie.'

" 'Why haven't you got any pictures of him?' I said. 'He's popular, isn't he?'

"Claudia said he'd dropped out of sight as soon as he arrived. He wasn't with his family. He wasn't at any of the city hotels. They had a report he'd been seen with a girl at Palm Beach, but they couldn't find him when they looked. Claudia said the word was he really did fancy Juliette a lot and wasn't playing for the PR people because of that. 'Quite sad,' she said. 'Lovely boy. Juliette's crazy. I'd drop that clapped-out Frere like a hot potato for him.'

" 'Clapped-out?' I said. 'He's gorgeous!'

"Birdie groaned of course, but Claudia just rolled her eyes at me. 'You're as bad as Juliette. She was bowled over when he made a line for her. No doubt about that. Oh well, she's a kid. She'll learn. They all do.' "

"Kate," Jeremy said patiently, "I can do without Claudia's world-weary philosophising. Is all this tripe leading anywhere?"

"Certainly. Just listen. The next day, yesterday, Claudia's baby was on the streets. She was over the moon. It was selling like hot cakes. Newspapers and magazines in the UK and US were bidding for the pool picture, everyone was talking about it. No one knew what Juliette thought about it. She was holed up in the hotel all day. So were Paul Frere and all the film people, and

Halkyn Spiers, so no one knew what he thought about it either. Her family still wouldn't talk.

"The premiere of *Flashpoint* was last night. Claudia was going. Once Birdie knew I was going to be alone, she came round, and we saw some of the arrivals on the late news, and taped it too, in case Claudia made an appearance. It was all very glam. But the smiles looked pretty strained to me. Halkyn Spiers looked quite fierce. I guess he didn't fancy being confronted with plain evidence that Juliette and Paul were having a real love affair. Juliette's father and sister weren't there at all. Juliette was all dolled up in this white lacy frock, with white stockings and tiny little high toe-peeper shoes and the whole ingenue bit. But when you looked at her tripping along so virginal and sweet, holding Paul Frere's arm so decorously, her topknot of black curls with little white flowers just brushing his chin as she turned to smile at people, as if he were a minder or a favourite uncle, you couldn't help thinking of that picture on the front of *Hers*. It spoiled the image, rather. And of course she knew it, and he knew it, and so did everyone else. The contrast was extraordinary.

"The item ended and I turned off the tape, and then I saw that Birdie was smiling all over her face. And when I asked her what was so funny, she just laughed. Then she said that, as she'd suspected, Claudia was full of shit and thought she knew it all but didn't. She said, 'Well, she might have won, as she puts it, on that sleazy cover shot. But she got diddled on the rest. Look at that! Plain as the nose on your face. What a joke!'

"I asked her what she was on about, of course. And of course she then went all smug and pointed at the TV and said why didn't I just play the tape again, and use my eyes and think about what I was seeing.

"So I did, and I looked, and I couldn't see what on earth she meant. She wouldn't tell me at first. But finally she did, after I promised and swore I wouldn't tell Claudia. Birdie wanted to do that her own way. After she'd really got hard evidence, she said, which she couldn't really get going till the morning.

"She got out the issue of *Hers* again, and turned to the inside pages. Juliette at the airport with family, Juliette and Paul playing peekaboo with the press in various picturesque locations, and so on. 'Look, dummy,' she said. 'Don't you see how bizarre all this is? We're supposed to believe that this couple wandered around barely touching, letting themselves be photographed doing nothing at all but talk for a week, just about. What on earth for? Why not touch? Why not go somewhere private? Didn't Juliette Nimmo say at the airport that all she wanted was peace and quiet, and to be alone?'

"I opened my mouth and she held up her hand. 'And don't repeat that Claudia garbage to me,' she said. 'Claudia's just too cynical for her own good. She's been diddled by a bimbo. She might have got her own back in the end, but that was just a fluke. Now, play the tape again and look at this!'

"She put her finger on the picture of Juliette and Paul at the fruit and vegetable market, and then pointed at the TV screen. 'Spot the difference,' she said. I said well, other than their clothes I couldn't see a difference. In both places they were smiling, though the premiere smiles weren't at all natural. In both she was turned slightly towards him, with the top of her head just brushing his chin. And then, finally, I saw it. There really wasn't a visible difference, but there should have been. At the market Juliette was wearing flat running shoes. At the premiere, on the TV screen, she was wearing those pretty little toe-peepers with very high heels. And yet in both pictures her height looked the same!

"Birdie pointed at the first photograph in the *Hers* lineup. Juliette, Alexandra and Frank Nimmo, smiling for the camera. As I'd noticed before, Alexandra Nimmo looked very like Juliette. Not as pretty, not as petite, but the same colouring. A perfect foil for her star sister in the picture. A perfect understudy for the press. It was obvious what had happened. Juliette and Paul and Juliette's family had organised the week of peace and quiet Juliette wanted. Alexandra took the week off work, moved into Juliette's suite at the Imperial and took her sister's place in the limelight. She mightn't have pulled it off on her own, but with Paul in tow no one would even think about it. The two of them had trailed the press around while Juliette went underground in absolute peace and privacy.

" 'No wonder they were so circumspect,' Birdie said, grinning in high delight. 'They hardly knew each other.'

" 'Must have been a bit odd for Alexandra, mustn't it?' I said. 'The high life at the Imperial, limos, great food, one of the most famous film stars in the world as your escort for a few days, and then back to the suburbs and dear old dad when sis comes back refreshed to reclaim her rightfuls.'

"Birdie said that anyone with sense would be mightily relieved, but there was no accounting for taste.

"It was only then that I started thinking about how red Claudia's face was going to be over all this. I was glad I'd promised not to tell her. She'd be devastated at being so fooled. Birdie swore me to secrecy again, and went off giggling. I went to bed, so I wouldn't have to face Claudia when she got home.

"This morning Claudia left bright and early and happy as a lark, if a bit hung-over. But about half-past nine she rang me at work with the news. Paul Frere had been found dead in his room at the Imperial. Suicide. She was in a terrible state. She'd already been contacted by a few papers wanting her comments. Was it possible the PR and family problems caused for Juliette by the pool picture had tipped him over the edge? She kept saying over and over how ridiculous that was, but there was no other reason for it, was there? Was there? Why on earth should he kill himself? True, he'd seemed a bit twitchy over the last few days, but the week before he'd been okay, and there was no reason for him to

suddenly go downhill. He wasn't drinking at the moment, everyone said. His last film had been a great success. He had Juliette.
But he'd done it. He'd taken an overdose of some narcotic in a
drink—not alcohol, some Chinese herbal health concoction he
apparently always had before going to bed. He'd kept that detail
of his daily routine a dead secret up to now. Probably he used the
stuff to help him get it up, she said, being Claudia and absolutely
incapable of not conjecturing on salacious details even in circumstances like this.

"Then an hour later she rang me again. Birdie had called in
to see her. With purely malicious intent, of course, but as it happened, for once it completely backfired. Claudia was over the
moon. There was one thing I hadn't really thought about last
night. If Juliette wasn't at the Imperial in those few days, where
was she? Claudia said she knew, and was about to prove it if she
had to bribe every person in Palm Beach to do it. And then the
motive for Paul Frere's sadness over the past week, and his subse-
quent suicide would be obvious for all to see. 'Sweetie, that Birdie
is *fabulous!*' she screamed at me before she rang off. I had to
laugh. Poor Birdie. She'd be furious."

Jeremy grinned. "It'll do her good," he said. "Well, didn't I
say that Nimmo was a bimbo?"

"She fooled everyone, didn't she? Not such a bimbo."

"Well, nasty piece of work, then. Poor old Frere does her a
favour and she grabs the chance to two-time him. Great, huh?"
He yawned.

Kate stood up and began clearing away the tea things. "Yeah.
Well, that's show business! Let's go to bed. You must be tired."

The doorbell rang. Groaning, Jeremy went to answer it.

Birdie stood expectantly on the doorstep. Her glasses glittered in the light of the streetlamp outside. "G'day. Just passing,
thought I'd drop in," she said to him nonchalantly, and walked
into the hall.

"It's ten o'clock, Birdie," Jeremy said. "It's no longer good day. Good night would be far more appropriate."

"I thought Kate might like to hear the end of our little drama. Did she tell you about it?"

"She told me you'd tried to embarrass Claudia and ended up helping her out, yes," said Jeremy nastily. But Birdie refused to be discomforted. She walked into the kitchen.

"How about a drink for an old digger?" she said to the astonished Kate. "And then I'll tell you how Claudia and I nailed a murderer this afternoon."

"*What?!*"

"I'm telling you. White wine?"

Kate wordlessly poured a glass of wine for the three of them. Birdie sipped hers with satisfaction. "Nice," she said appreciatively.

Jeremy could stand it no longer. "Okay, Birdwood," he said. "I'm tired. Tell. Now."

She smiled at him. "I called Dan Toby and told him Alexandra had stood in for Juliette for a week. I told him Claudia said Juliette had probably used her week to have a fling with Halkyn Spiers. She then went back to the Imperial, had a passionate reunion with Frere, and then after a day or two realised she preferred the young, hot Halkyn after all and told Frere it was all over. Motive for suicide established. Very neat. Toby told me that was great but there was just one little problem. They were pretty sure it wasn't suicide, but murder. The drink Frere always had tasted vile. His naturopath in the US told them he loathed drinking it. Why would he use it to put poison in, when he could have used alcohol or coffee, both of which were in his room? And he never used drugs of any kind, uppers or downers. The bottle found in his cupboard didn't have his fingerprints on it. It had been wiped clean. Someone with access to his suite put a drug in his drink, and killed him."

"But why should Juliette kill him?" exclaimed Kate. "She could have left him for Spiers easily, at any time."

"Stop jumping to conclusions. Of course she could. But there are lots of other possibilities. Lots of other people had access to that suite, because it adjoined Juliette's. What if Juliette *didn't* want to leave Paul Frere, with whom she always seemed genuinely in love, for Spiers? Spiers might have taken matters into his own hands, enraged by Claudia's pool passion picture. What if Daddy Nimmo was so outraged by the same picture that he decided to wipe out the corrupter of his innocent daughter? What if Alexandra Nimmo . . ."

"Got sick of playing second fiddle," said Kate slowly. "And decided to take away from her sister the only thing she really loved . . . again, the picture. Imagine how it must have felt, having to leave Frere, the Imperial, the glamour . . . like being cast out of paradise. And then seeing that photograph, her sister with everything she didn't have. That picture . . ."

Birdie smiled. "Oh, yes, the picture was the problem, all right. For Frere, and Juliette, Alexandra, Halkyn Spiers and Frank Nimmo. Because all of them were in on the secret of Juliette's week underground. All of them knew that the girl being photographed with Frere was Alexandra. All along. In the limo, at the Quay, at the market . . . and, lastly, the night before Juliette came back to reclaim her identity, by the pool."

"*What!*"

Birdie nodded and stretched. "It's clear as a bell, when you look at the whole pool series," she said. "Toby's got them now. The height thing's a complete giveaway. But even the one on the cover of *Hers* is plain enough, when you blow it up. The two girls are alike enough to pass muster at a distance, given that people see what they expect to see, and the photographer at the pool had been trailing the same couple for nearly a week, so of course it looked right to her. But Alexandra it is—in *all* the photographs.

Believe me. She's admitted it to Toby now, anyway, and filled in the gaps. She said she and Paul Frere fell in love, during their days together. He said she was fresh, and sweet, and beautiful, like Juliette used to be before Hollywood got her. He was going to leave Juliette for her. This time, at last, it was the real thing for him, he said."

"He always says that," said Kate scornfully. "Since his last divorce he hasn't stuck with anyone for more than a year. Juliette was the exception. Well, I suppose she wasn't, as it turns out."

"No. They were going to tell Juliette 'at the right time,' Alexandra says. When she got back from the health farm where she'd been, alone, they just pretended everything was fine. They didn't know they'd been photographed. The first they knew about it was when they saw that picture on the cover of *Hers* yesterday. They were panic-stricken. And then Juliette saw it too, just before they went off to the premiere of *Flashpoint*. She was . . . murderous, Alexandra says. Frere thought he could deal with her, but—apparently she dealt with him."

"She killed him!"

"Seems a sure thing. The drug he drank's the same as one prescribed for her. Toby's having a word with her now. If she's clever and keeps her mouth shut she might get off. But I don't think so."

"How's Alexandra?"

"Devastated. Thinks her life's over. But she'll come good. She's only a kid. And she's better off without Paul Frere. She'll probably see that in the end. And after all, she only knew him a week."

"A week's a long time in show business," said Kate drearily.

"And in magazines, apparently," grinned Birdie. "I left your mate Claudia tearing apart the cover of her next issue and jeering in print at her rivals for being hoodwinked!"

"But she was hoodwinked too!"

"Ah, yes, but she's rising above that. Great operator, that Claudia! You know she's offered me a job?"

Jeremy and Kate looked at each other. "Let yourself out, Birdie," Kate said. "We're going to bed."

They left her pouring a fresh glass of wine. Once they were gone she put her feet on the table, lit a cigarette, and reached for the *Hers* magazine. She turned to the back and began with the Stars.

DEATH IN RUBY

"WHAT D'YOU WANT TO GO out there for, love? I'm telling you, you won't get nothing out of Ted Sloan. Always was a surly young chap. There's nothing he can tell you about the bloody drought that a hundred people here in Ruby can't. I'm telling you, you could just sit here in the pub all day and there'd be enough blokes bending your ear about it to make twenty flaming TV shows." The man behind the bar shook his head and pushed a glass of beer towards the small woman facing him.

Verity Birdwood glanced thoughtfully at him. Her glasses flashed as they caught the light. "I'm supposed to interview someone who's getting ready to throw in the towel," she said. "I was told Ted Sloan was thinking of walking off his place. He's sold off all his stock, they told me."

"Yeah, well . . ." The hotel owner shifted uncomfortably. "You do what you like, Miss Birdwood—er, Birdie—but the Sloans have never liked people on the place. Old Cyril Sloan was a nasty piece of work, if you want the truth, and Ted's probably no better. Not that I've seen him for donkey's years. You just watch yourself, that's all I'm saying." He looked with attention at the glass he was polishing. "Shirley Perkins lives out that way. She'll probably give you a lift."

"Look, thanks for your help, Fred. And don't worry," said Birdie, grinning at him. "I'm just going to go out to Red Knob and ask. You say he doesn't answer the phone, so I can't call first. If he tells me to push off, I will. It's my job to have a go, though. You see?"

The man turned away and began stacking glasses. "Yeah," he said, more to himself than to her. "Well, you watch it."

Birdie bounced uncomfortably on the dusty seat of the utility. It was stiflingly hot. Dust rose on either side of them as the wheels roared on the red dirt road, and the country around them lay flat, bleached and parched under the remorselessly blue sky. Tufts of silvery grass lined the roadway, ringbarked trees stood up white like skeletons and crows watched from dry branches with cold eyes. "The Red Knob turnoff's up here on the left," said the woman at the wheel. Her plump, freckled forearms were glistening with sweat and the lurid floral of her polyester dress showed dark patches on her back and sides.

"This is very kind of you, Mrs. Perkins," said Birdie.

"Oh, well, it's on my way, love," said the woman casually. "I won't stay, though. I don't like that place. And I don't know Ted Sloan. Never seen him since he was a kid, and a proper little bugger he was then, excuse the French. Still . . ." she sniffed, "what would you expect, with a dad like that?"

"Everyone says that," said Birdie, watching her. "No one seems to have a good word to say for the old man. Why's that?"

"Well," Mrs. Perkins narrowed her eyes in the glare and a thousand lines appeared on her sun-dried face. "He was one of those people who's always out for himself. You know. Like, he bought Red Knob with a partner, Harry Lidcomb, thirty-five years ago. Both of them put money in, and both worked like dogs. Their wives too. Ann Lidcomb, Harry's wife, was a good friend of mine. I was godmother to their little Billy, as a matter of fact.

"The farm started to pay after a while, see, and pretty soon a half share wasn't good enough for Cyril Sloan. He started working on Harry."

Birdie looked at her curiously. "How?" she asked.

Mrs. Perkins hissed softly through closed teeth. "Oh, Harry was a nice bloke, but a weak sort of type, you know? It was easy. Few drinks of a night. Few games of cards. Few bets between them on the horses. Few more drinks. Few more bets. By the time Ann found out about it Harry was in up to his silly neck—owed Cyril Sloan thousands, and no way in the world to pay it back. Except one." She shook her head. "So Cyril and his wife and son got the farm, and Harry and Ann and their little Billy got to move away with no debts, and not a brass razoo to bless themselves with. It was wicked. Deliberate, greedy, planned wickedness." She tapped the steering wheel with stubby fingers. "Some people are devils," she said. "That woman who let Edie Sant rot in gaol for a murder she hadn't done! And look at what's-his-name . . . Burke, who—"

"What happened to the Lidcombs?" Birdie broke in, rather abruptly.

Mrs. Perkins stared at the road ahead. "I only heard from Ann twice, after," she said. "First time they were somewhere in Sydney. She didn't give the address. Harry was doing some labouring job. Then she wrote again to say Harry was dead. He'd killed himself." Mrs. Perkins' commonplace face tightened to a grim mask. "In her view, Cyril Sloan killed him. And as far as I'm concerned, she's right. Whatever happened to the old man six months ago, it was no more than he deserved."

"He had a stroke, didn't he?" said Birdie quietly.

"That's the story, yes," said Mrs. Perkins coldly. "Some hired bloke they'd got in knocked him down. He couldn't move or talk or nothing for four months. Then his heart failed and he died. Well," she glanced defiantly at Birdie, "you wouldn't wish it on a dog, would you? And I suppose you think I'm a callous old tart to say it. But when I think of Ann and all she went through, I can't find a grain of pity for him. I just can't."

The car thundered on. The fine red dust rose behind them like the smoke of a smouldering fire.

"Look, love, are you sure you're okay?" Mrs. Perkins rested her plump arm on the open window of the utility and squinted at the house beyond the last wire gate, with its crudely painted "No Trespassers" sign.

"Sure, Mrs. Perkins. I'll be all right," said Birdie. Her small, pointed face beneath its bush of brown hair looked pale in the fierce sunlight.

Mrs. Perkins threw the utility into reverse gear and looked around her. "Bone dry," she said. "Two years since we've had good rain. Look at that—the big dam's going. No wonder he had to get rid of his beasts."

Birdie looked down the hill and saw the great walls of bare red-brown earth sloping down to a thin sheen of oily water. A few crows flapped overhead.

"Tooroo, then." Mrs. Perkins turned the utility, its wheels making little sound on the soft dust of the track.

Birdie lifted an arm in farewell as the vehicle plunged back up the hill into a tunnel of its own dust, still hanging in the still air from the downward journey. Then she picked up her overnight bag and camera, and began trudging towards the silent house.

She remembered what Dan Toby had said, leaning over his

untidy desk in the crowded Sydney police headquarters, the day before she left for Ruby. "While you're there," he'd said, in his slow, deep voice, "see if you can get a look at Red Knob, Birdie. Six months it's been, and they're no further on up there. According to the son, Ted Sloan, a cove calling himself Sid Golds turned up one morning, looking for a job. Sloan says he left his father alone with Golds and went out to work. When he got back an hour and a half later, the old man was lying on the kitchen floor, unconscious, and Golds was gone, with some cash and some bits of jewellery that had belonged to Ted's mother. He rang town for help. Old man had had a stroke. No sign of Golds then and no sign of him now. No record of anyone by that name anywhere, as a matter of fact. No one saw the bloke arrive, and no one saw him leave."

Toby had shaken his head. "The thing is, Birdie, did some thug calling himself Sid Golds beat up an old man for a few dollars and go into smoke? Or is Sid Golds a convenient fiction? Not much love lost between the old bloke and his son, according to local gossip. But the truth is, no one really knows much about them. They're isolated out there at Red Knob. The mum died fifteen years ago. Kid was fifteen or sixteen then. He took off to the city pretty soon after, and only turned up again a couple of years ago. They kept themselves to themselves. The old man'd pick up food and petrol and stuff in town once a month. Only thing he ever said about his son, just after he got back, was that he was as much of a no-hoper as ever, and was hanging around so he could take over Red Knob when his father died. Then the old boy cracked a smile, apparently, and said he'd have a long wait." Dan Toby had paused and looked at the small woman leaning forward in her hard chair. "Not so long, as it happens," he'd said quietly.

· · ·

A dog barked half-heartedly as Birdie walked up to the house, past a rusty tank and dry gardens. The screen door creaked and a figure appeared in the dim doorway. Birdie shaded her eyes and peered up into the shadow.

"Hello!" she said. "Mr. Sloan, is it?"

The screen door squeaked again and a tall, dark woman appeared on the porch, slipping out of the shadowy house with a curiously furtive twist. Birdie put down her bag. "Oh, sorry," she began. "Sorry. I couldn't see."

"I'm Mrs. Sweeney, the housekeeper. He's not here," said the woman flatly. Her voice was harsh, with a curious grating quality to it.

"I need to talk to him. Could I possibly come in and wait?"

The woman shrugged. Her eyes were dark and ringed with grey. Her black hair was cropped short, framing unbecomingly her big-boned face, with its long chin and thin, pale lips. She stepped back, held the screen door open with one arm, and waited. A grim-looking personage, thought Birdie, raising her eyebrows. She picked up her bag and walked up the couple of stairs into the house.

"Actually, I thought Mr. Sloan lived here alone, Mrs. Sweeney." Birdie was trying to be chatty, but the woman wasn't helping. She stood silently by the old-fashioned sink, her large, red-knuckled hands, glistening with water, fumbling clumsily with potatoes and a blunt-looking knife.

"I came to look after Mr. Sloan's father, four months ago," she said dully, without looking around. "He'd just come back from hospital. Couldn't speak. Couldn't do anything for himself."

"It's a wonder they didn't keep him in hospital, where he could be looked after properly," said Birdie, without thinking.

The woman turned slowly and looked at her with dead,

deep-set eyes. "He got every care," she said. "I didn't neglect him, if that's what you mean."

"Oh, no . . ." Birdie hastily tried to repair the damage. "I just meant—most sons wouldn't want to take the responsibility."

The woman turned back to the sink. "Looking after the old man was my responsibility," she said. "Mr. Sloan didn't spend much time with him. Went in every night and sat with him a quarter of an hour or so, just looking. Never touched him or spoke to him that I saw. Then I'd have to get the old man off to sleep."

"Was that difficult?"

Mrs. Sweeney emptied the basin of muddy water, dried her hands on her apron, and turned her dead eyes towards Birdie again. She stood, tall and mannish, by the sink, her arms hanging loose. "Yes. He was hard to settle."

There was a heavy silence.

"Old Mr. Sloan died two months ago, I gather," Birdie said at last.

"Yes. I stayed on," said Mrs. Sweeney, answering the unstated question. "I'll stay till the place is sold. If it's sold. Who'd buy a pile of dust?"

A step sounded on the stair and the door was pushed open. A thin, dark, harassed-looking man with his right hand wrapped in a dirty crepe bandage stood in the doorway. Birdie braced herself, and rose to argue her case.

It was easier than she'd expected. After the first shock of seeing an intruder in the house, Ted Sloan seemed to accept her arrival and regard an overnight stay as inevitable. Maybe it was the resignation of the hopeless. Or maybe he'd been unfairly tarred by the townspeople of Ruby with the same brush as his irascible and greedy father. He sat now, staring at the empty grate in the stuffy living room. Mrs. Sweeney clattered dishes in the kitchen. He pulled out a packet of cigarette tobacco and began rolling a cigarette with his left hand, using his bandaged right hand only to press back straying, sticky brown strands.

"What happened to your hand?" asked Birdie.

The man jumped a little, pulling the bandaged hand closer to his chest. "I strained something. It started the day I . . . found my father lying in the kitchen," he muttered. "Tried to lift him too quickly, or something." His sunburned face, finely blistered on nose, forehead and cheekbones, was suddenly shining with sweat.

Birdie looked at him curiously. This man was very near to breaking point. "Mr. Sloan, I'm sorry if I'm keeping you from your work," she said quietly. "We can talk tonight, if you'd rather."

"No. No, it's all right," said the man, opening his eyes and swivelling them in her direction. "The work is pointless. I was just looking at the fences, before. But they can fall down, really, for all I care. There's no point in any of it. The heart's gone out of the place. Nothing but dirt and crows now."

They talked for an hour, in the dim sitting room. About the property, and the drought, and the gradual disintegration of hope. Strangely enough, the man seemed gradually to relax, as though talking about the tragedy was relieving an intolerable tension.

"You should have seen this place like I did when I was a kid," he was saying now. "I thought it was paradise on earth. I thought I'd live here forever." He smiled and stared at the empty grate.

"Did your father feel the same way?"

"Dad felt the same. It would've killed Dad to see it like this. I'm glad he never did." Abruptly he shook his head, dismissing the gentle thought.

"Have you seen the big dam?" It was Mrs. Sweeney, standing gaunt by the kitchen door. "It's dropped a handsbreadth since yesterday, I'd say. Tomorrow it'll be a puddle."

He slumped back. "That's impossible!" For a moment he stared into space. "Ah—what the hell, anyway."

"It'll never sell, this place." Around Mrs. Sweeney's thin lips a slight smile hovered. "Not like this." She went back into the kitchen, closing the door behind her.

"She's not very joyful company for you," said Birdie, to break the silence.

"Beggars can't be choosers," said the man. "She turned up on the doorstep looking for work. I was just about to advertise for someone to help with the old man. It seemed like fate. She's a bit of an oddball, but who wouldn't be if they were willing to work in a place like this?"

Birdie raised her eyebrows. "Turned up on the doorstep? Out here?"

He shrugged. "She must've heard there was a job going."

The old house creaked, and the hot, thick darkness pressed heavily on the bed where Birdie lay. She turned on her side and tried to settle her mind for sleep. A depressing household. And some strange anomalies. She thought back to the evening's conversation. The photograph album, filled with fuzzy, happy snaps; one picture in particular—"Cyril & Ted vs. Harry & Billy. Happy days!" it was titled, in neat, faded printing. Birdie had looked curiously at the photograph, trying to trace in the frozen faces the seeds of future loss and betrayal. Cyril Sloan, tall and balding, stood with his arms spread wide behind his skinny, dark son, who was getting ready to heave a cricket ball down the dusty road outside the house. At the other end of the improvised pitch stood a laughing, black-haired boy with a bat held at an impossible angle, like a baseball bat, behind his left shoulder. A quieter-looking man stood smiling there, his hand on his son's head. Birdie pointed to him.

"That's your father's partner, Harry Lidcomb, is it?"

"Ex-partner. Yeah."

"I suppose you were sorry when Billy left? Your playmate?"

He grimaced, shrugged. "I guess. I was only a kid."

"He'd be grown up now, wouldn't he? Would you know him now, if you saw him?"

The man stared at her. "God, no! It's been twenty years. Listen, why are you asking me about this? What've you heard?"

Birdie moved restlessly; the bed creaked, the house creaked. She thought of the slender fingers of the man's unbandaged hand running distractedly again and again through the thatch of dark hair. And the gentleness of his voice when he spoke about his father and the past. Could he conceivably have struck his father down in a moment of rage and then, appalled, made up the story of the mystery man Sid Golds and cared for the paralysed old man, with the help of the odd Mrs. Sweeney, till he died? Too ashamed to touch him. Too stricken to talk to him. But drawn, evening after evening, to his room? It could have been like that, and yet . . .

Look at it the other way. Birdie moved restlessly under the single sheet that covered her. Say Ted Sloan was innocent. Where, then, was the guilty Sid Golds? Where in these denuded hills, these barren roads, had he hidden, that first day? Where was he now? Was the attack on the old man made for the sake of a few trinkets and some ready cash? Or was there another reason, a reason that lay far deeper, and cast much longer shadows?

Images began to blur as they floated through Birdie's mind in the hot darkness. Four happy faces, playing cricket . . . "Cyril & Ted vs. Harry & Billy" . . . Mrs. Perkins' flushed, stern face . . . "wicked. Deliberate, planned wickedness" . . . the sad, sun-blistered, uncertain face of Ted Sloan, looking into the empty grate . . . the closed, shadowed face of Mrs. Sweeney. The faces, the images, circled, changed places, made patterns, like a kaleidoscope. And suddenly, without warning, they clicked into a shape that made Birdie open her eyes and sit up. She breathed quietly, thinking it through. It all fitted. Slowly, she lay back on the pillow. Now she could sleep. She knew.

In the morning Birdie entered the kitchen quietly, nodded to the silent figure by the stove, the man drinking tea at the table. Already the heat was building.

"I thought I'd get a few photographs outside, if that's okay," she said. "Before it gets too hot."

He shrugged. "Whatever you like. It doesn't matter."

"I'll go to the big dam first."

He smiled his weary, bitter smile and raised his eyebrows, but said nothing. She left him sitting at the table and went outside. As she looked back, the tall figure of Mrs. Sweeney moved to close the door, to shut out the heat and light.

Birdie stood at the edge of the dam. Caked mud, imprinted with the slotted marks of hundreds of vanished sheep, sloped down to the merest slick of muddy water. Crows hopped on its margins and watched her with yellow eyes. And half in, half out of the water, sprawled with grotesque, ungainly grace in the baking sun, lay something that had been a man before the water, and the yabbies, and now the crows, had changed it into something else.

Then she heard the shot. She turned and raced for the house, knowing her haste was pointless, knowing what was waiting for her there.

She ran past the tank, up the dusty steps, in through the squeaky screen door. He was in the living room, slumped in the armchair by the cold fireplace. The photograph album lay open on his lap, and blood dripped from the shattered side of his head.

Mrs. Sweeney stood, absolutely motionless, beside him. She turned her head slowly as Birdie entered the room. Her exhausted eyes moved to the rifle she held in her hand, to the red stains that smeared her big hands. She lifted the gun.

"Not again," she breathed. "Please, not again. Don't come any closer."

Birdie stepped forward calmly and took the rifle from her unresisting fingers. "Sit down, Mrs. Sant," she said. "It is Edie Sant, isn't it?"

The woman crumpled on to the couch, her face in her hands.

"I know it wasn't you, Mrs. Sant." Birdie spoke quietly, insistently.

"Was it—was it Golds?" The whites of the woman's eyes showed, and she looked fearfully around the shadowy room.

"There is no Golds," said Birdie.

"Then . . . then he . . . did it himself?" The woman glanced unbelievingly at the still figure in the chair. "And *he* attacked his father? But the way he talked, about the old days, his father . . . I thought . . ."

"I know. He loved his father all right. And he loved this place. That's why he killed. Twice. And now he's killed himself."

The woman moved helplessly. "I don't understand."

"I've been to the big dam," Birdie said carefully. "He knew what I'd find."

"What you'd . . ." Horror began to grow on the woman's gaunt face. "What do you mean?"

"There's someone there. He's been dead a long time."

"Golds?"

"There was no Golds."

"Who, then?"

Birdie thought of the grinning wreck of bones and rotted flesh sprawled half in, half out of the muddy water. She looked at her hands. "He'll have to be looked at. But I think . . . I'm sure . . . it's Ted Sloan."

The woman stared at her, mouth hanging open. Then she turned her head again to look at the quiet figure slouched in the armchair. "But that's Ted."

"No," said Birdie slowly. "That's Billy Lidcomb. He's been settling some old scores."

They sat for a moment, and the blood tapped steadily on the photograph album. On the picture of some people playing cricket on a dusty road. "Cyril & Ted vs. Harry & Billy. Happy days!"

Dan Toby looked at the small woman who sat composed and a little scruffy on the other side of the desk.

"So," he rumbled. "Got your story and sorted it all out for us, did you?"

She shrugged. "It wasn't very hard. He was at the end of his tether anyway. He'd had this dream of quietly living on the place he saw as rightfully his—that his father had been cheated of. But it didn't work out. I don't know, maybe he'd only meant to confront the Sloans, and demand his rights, but the meeting ended with the old man unconscious and Ted Sloan dead. He put Ted in the dam, with a few bits of jewellery from the bedroom. He'd done his homework, presumably, and knew no one had seen Ted Sloan close up since he was a kid. He couldn't see any reason why he couldn't just step into the dead man's shoes.

"It all went like clockwork at first. Anyway, no one suspected he wasn't Sloan, not for a moment. But he found murder wasn't as easy to forget as he'd thought. Ted's body in the dam must have haunted him. And the old man didn't die. He had to bring him home, in case he ever talked and spilled the beans. The drought didn't break. The land was blowing away. And the big dam started drying up. He knew it was only a matter of time, especially when I turned up. But, I didn't think he'd . . ." She looked up at Toby and her amber eyes were blank behind the thick glasses.

"You can't blame yourself, Birdwood," Toby said impatiently. "He could've cracked any time, with you or without you. How'd you guess he wasn't Sloan, anyhow?"

"I didn't guess, Dan. I worked it out," said Birdie, with a touch of asperity. "I saw a photograph of the two fathers and their sons playing cricket. He wasn't scared to show it to me. Two little kids, both dark-haired and skinny, blurry picture, all that. He could have been either one. But young Billy was a left-hander. He was batting left-handed, anyway. And I'd noticed that the bloke who said he was Ted Sloan was a left-hander too, but pretending that he wasn't. He was pretending that he'd injured his right hand. That way, you see, he could sign all the necessary papers with his bandaged hand, and just approximate Ted's signature, and also keep the use of the hand that was really vital to him in everyday life—the left. He was much too clever with his left hand though, for me to be fooled. Rolled a cigarette left-handed right in front of me.

"Then, I saw that Cyril Sloan had been bald. Balding badly, and he was quite young in the photograph. Baldness is usually hereditary. But the man calling himself Ted Sloan had thick hair still, like Harry Lidcomb in the photograph. He was badly sun-burned, too, which was odd for a man who was supposed to have been running a farm for a couple of years."

Dan Toby shook his head. "It's clever, Birdie. But it's flimsy. You couldn't have been sure. And you'd never have proved it without the body in the dam."

"I knew it was there," said the small woman composedly. "There or somewhere else close by. And I was sure, all right. The man I met didn't fit the picture of Ted Sloan, who was a 'little bugger' as a child, who was 'surly,' who fought with his father. He was sensitive and emotional, and loving. He told me how he'd always loved the place, how his father had loved it. He said, 'It would've killed him to see it like this. I'm glad he never did.' But that part of the country's been drought-stricken for years. If he'd really been Ted Sloan, the remark wouldn't have made sense. But if he was Billy Lidcomb, it made all the sense in the world."

Toby sighed, and flicked the papers on his desk. "Can't help feeling sorry for him, can you?" he said.

Birdie looked at him. "I keep thinking, though, about the old man."

"Who? Cyril Sloan?"

"Yes. Lying there in his own house, aware, helpless and unable to tell anyone that the man who sat beside him every night wasn't his son but his son's killer, and his enemy. It must have been—like living in hell."

"Yes."

They sat in silence a while. Finally Toby cleared his throat. "Anyhow, something good's come out of all this."

"Edie Sant?"

"Yes. She's back in Sydney now. With her sister. She'll be all right, I think. Says she feels as though she's woken up after a nightmare. The shock, I suppose. Being found with a rifle, covered in blood—that's how it happened before, you know, with her husband. The jury didn't believe for a minute she'd picked up the gun after the event. Six years in gaol, Birdie, and then the dead man's girlfriend admits to the murder because she's got cancer and wants to make peace with God, or something. Lord! The things that happen to people. No wonder Edie dropped out and went bush after they let her out."

"I recognised her quite late on, really. She'd changed a lot from the photographs I'd seen. You know, I even played with the idea that she was the mysterious Sid Golds, at one stage. I'd already decided Golds could have been Billy Lidcomb. I thought maybe he'd dressed up as a woman to get back into the house and finish what he'd started. But . . . we all make mistakes."

"So we do." Toby stirred himself and grinned at her. "Come on," he said. "I'll buy you lunch."

They went out together into the familiar streets. The noise, the crowds, the humid Sydney heat engulfed them. And in another world, way out west in Ruby, Shirley Perkins sat crying on her verandah, watching the rain begin to fall.

ROSES FOR DO-HOPPY

DO-HOPPY'S DEATH DIDN'T MAKE the front pages.

A tiny paragraph on page eight of the late final edition marked his passing. And Do-Hoppy himself wouldn't have thought it worth a mention, thought Verity Birdwood, as she crossed Jervis Street to his corner of Jervis and Greeve. The old newspaper seller had stood there for as long as she could remember, croaking shorthand news of death, destruction, war, plague and murder. Familiar old buildings came down, taller, glossier buildings went up; streets became plazas; boutiques bloomed and died like spring flowers; the sound of jackhammers drowned out the city's subtler human sounds. But Do-Hoppy, small and wizened of face, chanting the news of the moment, doling out papers obsolete in half a day, had seemed a fixture. The city seemed the poorer without him.

She forgot herself so far as to express this thought to the big man who picked his way beside her through the narrow obstacle course that both sides of Greeve Street had become in recent months while yet more shopping complexes were constructed on the block. Detective Sergeant Dan Toby took his eyes from his feet for a moment to glance at her in amusement.

"The sentimental Birdwood. Now there's something you don't see every day," he drawled, and tripped on a piece of pipe sticking out unaccountably from the hoarding that screened the footpath from the road. "Oh, blast!" He hopped on the spot in ungainly fashion, rubbing his ankle.

"Serves you right, you callous bastard," snapped Birdie irritably, dodging around him. "Poor harmless old bloke gets it in the neck and you make a joke of it. And you're doing bugger-all about getting the pig who did it. All too hard, is it?"

"God, you're offensive when you like," growled Toby. "What d'you want? It only happened this morning. But you know as well as I do we've got an iceberg's chance in hell of getting anywhere. We know it was early—the old man hadn't even finished setting up. He was always in action by seven, so we reckon between six-thirty and, say, five to seven. Hardly anyone about here at that time of day. He was thumped on the back of the head with a brick and his bag was nicked and anyone at all could've done it. No witnesses, or at least none that we can find. No one sees past their bloody noses in the city. The flower stall bloke opposite on this street reckons he couldn't see a thing because of a double-parked truck. The frock shop he stood outside wasn't open. The Jervis Hotel people across the way were changing guard or whatever they do at that time of day and they're no help. What are we supposed to do? We've got nothing to go on. It was simple robbery. Some mindless junkie after cash. Nothing to do with poor old Do-Hoppy, or whatever his name was, personally. End of story."

Birdie hesitated, glanced at him, and stopped dead. "Look, Dan, I've just thought of something," she said urgently. "Come back to the corner with me."

But Toby had had enough. "Birdie, for God's sake, forget it! I've had a bloody tiring day if you haven't. Do you want that drink, in which case I'll have it with you, or do you want to play cops and robbers, in which case you can do it on your own?" He glared at her in the failing light. People pushed impatiently past, heads down. Cars crawled bumper to bumper up and down Greeve Street beside them.

The small woman stared at him for a moment, then pushed her glasses back on her nose, and shrugged. "Okay," she said, "whatever you say." She started walking again, leading the way to the pub on the corner that remained mercifully unchanged at the end of the long trail of ruin and regeneration that was Greeve Street.

Dan Toby followed, uneasily aware that now he couldn't ask her, without loss of dignity, what it was she'd thought of in the matter of Dougal Joseph Hopkins, aka Do-Hoppy the paper seller. He could only hope that it was unimportant in the scheme of things.

The next morning found Birdie following her familiar track up Greeve Street two hours earlier than usual. The city always seemed very different in the early light. Hardly anyone about; a few cars speeding uninhibited through the deep shadows on the road. A solitary man tramped stolidly along on the other side of the road, staring straight ahead. No point in anything else. The shops had been entirely demolished for a month, and a wooden hoarding masked the growing excavation that had replaced tobacconist, hamburger joint and failed old family department store.

The few shops remaining on this side of the street were dark caverns at the end of little tunnels created by scaffolding and canvas. The Blue Lagoon, where Birdie always stopped for coffee, was firmly shut. She felt a stab of irritation, smiled at herself and shook her head. God, I'm getting set in my ways, she thought. Just start me off and I follow the same track to work like one of those old draught horses who can do the bread round without the driver. I get off the bus at the station, I cross at the lights to Greeve Street, I cross again to this side of Greeve Street and up I walk every bloody day! I've been doing it for years. Why don't I ever walk on the other side of the road? I could easily cross higher up, at Jervis or one of the other cross streets. It's just habit.

She thought about it, annoyed by the idea that she could be capable of irrationality. Then she saw that it was all, in fact, quite logical. There had never been a decent cafe on the other side of the road on this block. Only the greasy-spoon-type takeaway shop specialising in hamburgers, giant yellow doughnuts and finger buns. She liked decent coffee, and she liked to buy it at the first opportunity, so she always walked on this side of the road. Not so irrational, then. A matter of efficiency. Probably the man trudging along on the other side preferred watery coffee and yellow dough-nuts, and hadn't bothered to change his beat when the Greasy Spoon subsided into cockroach-ridden rubble.

A sharp gust of wind swept down Greeve Street, and she pulled her jacket more firmly closed. One windy, rainy winter morning years ago, on some sudden impulse, she'd bought a takeaway coffee for Do-Hoppy, she remembered. He'd seemed so taken aback by her gift that she felt as though she'd been guilty of overfamiliarity, and broken some unwritten rule of their long, formal street acquaintance. He'd taken the cup from her in his skinny brown hand, squinted at it shortsightedly, then limped in that jerky, hopping way of his to the other end of his stand and gingerly put the coffee down behind it, next to the wall. Then he'd limped back and peered at her under his eyebrows to see what she'd do next. Embarrassed, she'd just pushed her money into his hand, let him flick the folded newspaper under her arm as usual, and escaped into the crowd jostling across Jervis Street at

the lights, resisting the impulse to look back and see if he was
staring after her.

She had no way of knowing if he ever drank the coffee,
because he never mentioned it again, and she had never risked a
second attempt to warm him up on a rainy morning. But it was
from that day that their real acquaintance dated. After that, Do-
Hoppy, previously monosyllabic and businesslike in his dealings,
began to talk to her.

"You're a long time dead, aren'tcha?" he'd shocked her by
saying the following morning. He shoved her paper under her
arm and jerked his head scornfully after a sports car that had
screamed off from a standing start at the lights beside him, greedy
for every second saved. "What's the rush? You're a long time
dead." He looked at her under his eyebrows. She nodded and
muttered agreement, bemused by this development in their relationship.

"Work up yonder, do ya?" he went on, cocking his head
knowingly. "Up the ABC?"

"Yeah, that's right," said Birdie, wondering how he knew.

He cackled with satisfaction. "I seen you go in there one
Sat'dy last year. Anyhow, knew you were a journo minute I set
eyes on you." He cackled again at her surprise. "Old Do-Hoppy
don't miss much."

And so she learned his name, and his main source of pride.
Do-Hoppy, for his part, was reinforced in the unshakeable belief
that she was a news journalist, since she hadn't the heart to tell
him his instinct was awry and she was a researcher in quite a
different department. Unfortunately for her, many of their chats
from then on revolved around the story leads and underworld
gossip he seemed to pick up from myriad unsavoury acquain-
tances and was avid to share with a friendly, down-at-heel hack
who obviously needed a career boost. She always thanked him
and went off feeling guilty. At first she had attempted to pass

these tips on to the proper ABC quarters, but apparently Do-Hoppy's nose for news was not as keen as he believed it to be, and the amusement or bemusement with which her offerings were received soon discouraged her from persisting.

Birdie reached Do-Hoppy's corner and glanced at the empty place against the wall where the old man had stood in all weathers for so many years with his stand and his stacks of papers and magazines. No one had come to take his place. Presumably someone would. But not yet. Not today. And lying incongruously on the pavement, cellophane flapping in the draught created by passing cars, lay a bunch of roses.

Birdie went over to look at them. Eight red rosebuds in a cone of cellophane. Roses for Do-Hoppy. Who had put them there? She glanced around. There were a few early birds on the street now, busily and purposefully moving along their accustomed tracks to work, generally looking to neither right nor left, watching their feet on the boarded-up pavement. Occasionally one would glance at the space where Do-Hoppy should have been, hesitate with hand in pocket or purse, frown slightly and move on to the traffic lights paperless, no doubt suffering that little twinge of regret she had noticed when her morning coffee routine was interrupted. No one was paying any attention to the roses. She stuck her hands in her jacket pockets and stared at them, then slowly turned to look across Greeve Street where a flower seller was poking disconsolately among his bunches of blooms on the deserted pavement, his back to the road.

Behind her the boutique was dark. Shoe shop too. She knew those shops and the people in them, had sometimes seen them opening up as she passed. Across Jervis Street, behind its sweeping lay-by and elaborate entrance the Jervis Hotel was quiet, the tourists and business-trippers still breakfasting, presumably, or sleeping off heavy nights out with "Do Not Disturb" signs on their doors. As she watched, the bored-looking commissionaire loitering by the heavy glass doors was joined by another. Both men wore pale grey uniforms, gloves, and caps decorated with lavish ropes of gold braid. They stood side by side for a moment, arms folded, staring severely out into the street. The swords were missing, but otherwise they looked so exactly like some '30s Hollywood director's idea of romantic military that a song and dance seemed by no means out of the question. The scene must have been very like this yesterday morning when Do-Hoppy met his death so unobtrusively, slumping down into the narrow space between the back of his stand and the section of tiled wall dividing the boutique from the shoe shop next door. He must have been reaching behind the stand for extra stock, the police said, and been thumped from behind. Probably never knew what hit him.

There were things about all this that didn't ring true, Birdie thought. The killer had taken a terrible risk. Even with all the building and confusion around this area, and the earliness of the hour, the chances of getting away without being seen weren't great. The flower seller and the Jervis commissionaire were potential witnesses, for a start, let alone stray passers-by. You wouldn't think a paper seller's float worth the risk, for after all he hadn't started business yet, and his leather pouch wouldn't have contained much in the way of real cash. Some crazy, desperate junkie, Toby had said. Someone who was incapable of thinking the thing through just saw a helpless old man with money and went for him. Well, maybe. But last night, walking down Greeve Street, Birdie had remembered something. Something Do-Hoppy had said to her the morning before. She hadn't taken much notice of it at the time, but in the light of the old man's death . . .

"Got a story for ya," Do-Hoppy had muttered conspiratorially in her ear, as so often before. He'd cackled as he thrust the paper under her arm. "I seen a ghost this morning! Walking and talking, large as life. What d'ya think of that?"

She'd grinned, to show him she understood he was being humorous.

He'd sniggered again. "Think I'm joking, don'tcha? Well, the joke's on me, right? Wouldn't read about it. Give me an awful shock. 'Bugger me, here's trouble!' I says. 'I heard you was dead!' I says. And him! Near had a heart attack. 'You!' he says. 'Bloody Do-Hoppy!' White as a flaming ghost, anyhow, he was. 'By God,' he says. 'I never recognised you. An' it must be five years. God almighty!'

" 'More like ten years, mate,' I says. 'Ah well, so you're alive and kicking. There'd be a few interested to know that little lot.' And he wasn't too keen on that, I'll tell ya. That put the wind up him, all right! 'Never mind, mate,' I says to him. 'You know what I always used to say in the old days. Never trouble trouble till trouble troubles you.' Ah, he didn't like that either. 'You keep your mouth shut,' he says, and bolts like a scalded cat!" And Birdie remembered how the old man had grinned with delighted malice.

She'd smiled back at him, then, and started to turn away. The traffic lights at the crossing were about to turn green.

"Hey! Don'tcha want the story?" he'd croaked after her. "You haven't heard the real joke! I didn't get the strength of it meself till I saw what he did then. Blow me down if he doesn't—"

"I'm a bit late, Do-Hoppy," she said hurriedly. "I've got to catch the lights. I've got a meeting. I'll see you tomorrow."

The animation faded from his face. He shrugged, and hitched at his leather pouch.

"Suit yerself," he mumbled.

"Tomorrow, Do-Hoppy, for sure. Take care." Birdie lifted a hand in farewell, and he flicked a finger in grudging response.

She crossed at the lights, feeling uncomfortable. She didn't like to disappoint him.

But she was late, in fact. She'd listen to him properly tomorrow.

But, of course, by the time she got to his corner the next day, he was dead. Coincidence? Possibly. But she didn't think so.

Raised voices across Greeve Street caught her attention. The silver-haired flower seller was shouting in Italian at a younger man who had picked up a couple of buckets flaring with blooms and was standing at the lights waiting to cross, occasionally yelling impatiently back over his shoulder.

The lights changed and Birdie stood back as the man hurried across the road with his burden. He was stocky and dark, older than he had appeared at a distance. He plumped the buckets down beside her, in the space where Do-Hoppy's stand had stood, kicking the bunch of roses to one side as he did so.

The old man opposite shouted at him again, and he shouted back, then winked at Birdie. "Old man's got no sense," he said. "The space is free, right? Why not use it while we can? No good on our side anymore."

"Why not?" asked Birdie, watching with fascination as the flower seller opposite raged impotently, unable to bring himself to abandon his stand and pursue his errant assistant.

A woman trotting up to the lights spied the buckets, dug in her purse and bought a bunch of daisies. She sprinted off looking pleased with herself.

"See?" said the intruder. He bit his thumb insolently at his helpless employer still standing without custom beside the official stand, then turned back to Birdie.

"That corner's useless now. No cigarettes, no food, nothing since the shops down below went. The crowds come up this side now. Get their ciggies and takeaway and coffee from the Blue

Lagoon, see, and come on up and cross Jervis here. We're stuffed. I told my old dad-in-law over and over. But he's scared of the law."

He broke off to serve another two customers. "There," he said, shaking his head. "Three sales in five minutes. Nothing over there. See that?"

Birdie nodded. She watched him sell yet another bunch of daisies.

The old man across the road could stand it no longer. He grabbed his money pouch in both hands, plunged for the lights and made it, wheezing, to their side of Greeve Street, narrowly escaping being run down by a courier on a bike in the process.

"Johnny, you come back," he spluttered. "I told you. We got a licence. We got to stay put. You get me into trouble!"

"Four sales I made, Dad, in a few minutes here. What you done? Bugger all."

"This here's Do-Hoppy's place. We're not allowed here. You come back."

"He's not here anymore, Dad. He's dead." The young man jerked his head at the bunch of roses lying tattered on the foot-path. "You put them there?"

The old man hesitated. "What if I did, anyhow? I got a right. My friend. My roses."

"He's dead, Dad. What's the point?"

The flower seller's mouth tightened. He shrugged.

Birdie stepped forward. "You didn't see anything, yester-day?"

The old man's eyes narrowed. "I told the police . . . you a newspaper girl?"

"No, just a friend of Do-Hoppy's."

The old man shrugged again. "All the trucks, trucks in the way. I never saw nothing."

Johnny tapped his eyes significantly. "Getting on, you know?" he muttered to Birdie.

"What about you, then?" Birdie asked.

Johnny turned away to rearrange his remaining bunches of flowers. "Better bring over some more daisies, Dad," he said. "No, I didn't see because I wasn't here yesterday morning. Only started work with my father-in-law this week, and I had a few things to do at home before I came yesterday."

The old man snorted. "Few things! Few more hours' sleep, that's what you had to do. Why don't you stay home, anyhow? Leave me alone. I been here since before you got long pants on. I know what I do." Johnny sighed, smoothed his hair, rolled his eyes at Birdie. "We got to make the stand pay, Dad," he said reasonably. "I got to help you. Gabrielle told you, remember? Now look, you go get some more daisies, and another couple of mixed wrapped, okay? Cops come, I'll handle it."

"Johnny . . ."

Birdie left them to it and wandered across the road to the Jervis Hotel. The commissionaire stood, big and imperturbable, by the door. He began to swing it open for her. Birdie decided to come straight to the point.

"I was a friend of the old guy who sold newspapers across the road. Did you hear he was killed?"

The commissionaire allowed the door to swing gently closed again. He did it quite politely, but giving the distinct impression that people who regarded newspaper sellers as friends were not going to be at home in the marble and brass of the Jervis interior.

"We heard he was robbed and killed. Poor old chap," he said, his eyes flicking down to her shoes. Obviously he didn't approve of them, because he drew himself up and away from her very slightly.

"I was just wondering if you saw anything. It seems so strange that no one did."

"We did speak to the police. I relieve the night commissionaire at seven. Neither of us saw anything unusual." He pushed his
cap back slightly and for the first time his formal manner eased.
"Charlie and I were just talking about it this morning. We've both
been here years, on the same shifts, and I suppose you get out of
the habit of taking notice of people like that and their doings. He's
always been there. Ever since I've been here. Little chap in a cap.
Could've been anybody. Part of the furniture. Like Angelo on the
other side, the flower chap. I hardly notice what he's up to, either.
But for years I've walked up from the station and past his stand,
crossing Jervis there and then crossing Greeves to come on here.
You get into habits, don't you?"

"Yes. I was thinking that myself." So the commissionaire was
a yellow doughnut eater. He looked it. Birdie gazed across the
road. Johnny the interloper stood his ground with his buckets of
flowers, doing a brisk trade in daisies. On the opposite corner she
could just see old Angelo, hovering by his stand. Cars and trucks
growled by, masking her view and obscuring it completely when
they stopped at the lights. It was getting later now. By this time
yesterday morning Do-Hoppy had been an hour dead.

"Funny . . ." The commissionaire was warming up now. But
Birdie had another question. "Did you by any chance see anything unusual the day *before* yesterday? Anything at all?"

He looked at her suspiciously. "The day *before* yesterday?
What's that got to do with it? Look, I don't want to get involved in
any—"

"No, no, of course you don't," soothed Birdie hastily. "It's
not really important, or anything. Just curiosity really, but . . ."
She decided to risk a lie in the cause. "The flower seller—Angelo,
is it?—mentioned something, and I thought you might . . . ?"
She trailed off in what she hoped was an inviting manner.

The commissionaire stared at her in surprise for a moment,
and then his face cleared, and he grinned. "Ah, I see what you're

getting at. Yes, well, there was nothing in it, as you say, but I did see it, yes. Made me smile."

Birdie hesitated. This would be delicate. "Could you tell me exactly what happened? Angelo's accent's a bit much for me. I couldn't see the joke, really."

The big man grinned again. "Well, as to joke, it depends which way you look at it, you see. But it tickled me for sure. I was walking up Greeve Street, from the station, and I saw Angelo's new assistant, or whatever he is, cross from the other side of the road and try to set up shop next to the newsstand. Well, the old . . . the old man that's passed on wasn't having any of it. Trundled up and took him on eyeball to eyeball." He paused, and smiled reminiscently.

"Did you hear what they said?" Birdie asked, crossing her fingers.

He shook his head. "No, I was still too faraway to hear, but the old man scared the other one off all right. That bloke went off with a flea in his ear, I can tell you that. Picked up his buckets of daisies and bolted back across the road as fast as he could go, with a face like thunder. He was back with Angelo before I got to the newsstand corner." The commissionaire's grin broadened. Then he suddenly seemed to recollect the dignity of his official position and stopped smiling. "It was dangerous," he said pompously. "The building work makes the corner hazardous as it is. No room for more clutter."

He sprang to open the door for a heavily tanned American couple who emerged, blinking, into the morning sunlight and asked for a taxi. He produced a whistle, blew it, and beckoned importantly at the traffic. A taxi magically disengaged itself from the flow, sped into the lay-by and drew up beside them. Birdie slipped away. She wanted to get to work, and ring Dan Toby.

. . .

"Where've you been?" Toby demanded fretfully when she got through to him with far more speed than she expected. "I've been trying to get you all morning."

"It's only eight-thirty, Dan. I've just got here."

"You weren't at home either. Anyhow, you're here now. Look, last night, what were you going to say about Dougal Hopkins? The paper seller. Do-Hoppy. Are you there?"

"Yes, of course I am. Why do you want to know now? You didn't yesterday."

His gusty sigh huffed through the phone. "Look, don't give me a hard time, all right? As it happens, his money bag's been found in a bin in Hyde Park, wrapped in newspaper. The whole float's still in it. Looks like robbery wasn't the motive at all."

Birdie's throat tightened. So she was right.

"Well?" Toby's voice crackled with impatience. "What've you got for me?"

"You need to look for a man, maybe a crim, who Do-Hoppy knew well by sight up to about ten years ago. Someone who's supposed to be dead."

"What?"

"You heard me."

"Well, that's a fat lot of good, Birdwood. Your little mate knew a lot of people, didn't he? On both sides of the law. And an awful lot of people have died in the last ten years, in case you haven't noticed. Talk about a needle in a haystack!"

"Not quite that, Dan. There's more." And Birdie went through her story. After she had finished there was silence at the other end of the line.

"Dan?"

"I'm thinking. Well, it's a theory. Farfetched, like most of your theories, but . . ."

"Dan, I know I'm right. Look, just check it out, will you? Have I ever led you wrong?"

"Frequently."

"That's not fair. Anyway, this time I'm not asking you to do anything but check. That won't cause you any trouble, will it? Someone Do-Hoppy knew, who is supposed to be dead but could conceivably be alive, using another name, and who wouldn't want it known. Right?"

"Right, God help me."

"And ring me and tell me what happens, will you?"

"Oh, yes. Yes. Shouldn't be long. A couple of weeks, give or take a month."

The phone clicked as Toby rang off. Birdie put down the receiver and sat back in her chair. He was right. It was going to be almost impossible to get a name they could be sure of out of what she'd told him. And without it they'd have to take a real chance, because there was no evidence. If only there was some other clue, anything, in what Do-Hoppy had said on that last morning that would help. If only she'd listened more carefully, let him tell it all! She took off her glasses, closed her eyes and ran again through his story. She'd rehearsed it so often in the last twenty-four hours she could repeat it by heart.

. . . seen a ghost this morning . . . here's trouble, I says . . . my God, he says . . . never recognised you . . . five years . . . a few interested to know . . . put the wind up him . . . never trouble trouble till trouble troubles . . .

Birdie opened her eyes. She put on her glasses and reached for the phone. Toby answered on the second ring.

"It's me," she said. "Just a thought. That guy who took off with the half million about ten years ago. The getaway car driver, you know, who left his mates standing for the cops and just . . ."

"Yeah, Murphy. Thomas Murphy. Silly bugger. Panicked. Car went over the Gap."

"But they never found a body, did they? Or the money?"

"No. But that doesn't mean . . . What are you getting at, Birdie? Why Murphy?"

"Didn't he have a nickname?"

Toby paused. "They used to call him Trouble. Very apt. Big ugly brute with a record as long as your arm. But he's dead, Birdie. He's dead."

Birdie smiled. "No he's not, Dan. Yesterday he killed poor old Do-Hoppy. And right now he's whistling up taxis at the Jervis Hotel. Let's go and get him."

It was getting dark as Birdie walked with Toby down Greeve Street. Outside the Jervis Hotel a uniformed figure stared out into the street, no doubt unnerved by his abrupt recall to duty upon the arrest of his friend Tom, a nice chappie who had turned out to be not at all what he seemed. Old Angelo and his troublesome son-in-law had packed up for the night, and Do-Hoppy's corner was bare except for the bunch of roses still lying tattered by the wall.

"I knew it was him. The commissionaire. Logic told me that. But God, what a stroke of luck we could *prove* he was Do-Hoppy's ghost," said Birdie. "Once his fingerprints matched your file prints for Trouble Murphy . . ."

"The whole thing was bloody luck," Toby growled. "I admit it all worked out, with Do-Hoppy living next door to him in that boarding house years ago and all that. And he's confessed. No problem. Did I tell you, as well, that he's been dealing out of the Jervis? Literally had the stuff on him when he was nabbed. A bad lot all right. But just having a feeling about someone isn't logic, woman!"

Birdie stopped in her tracks. "It had nothing to do with having a feeling, you old twerp," she said rudely. "I've been through it all once! Look, it was plain as day from what Do-

Hoppy said that he was talking to someone he thought he hadn't seen for ten years. But the person he was talking to said, 'I never recognised you. And it must be five years. God almighty!' That sounded like the two of them had actually been at close quarters for years without recognising each other. Angelo the flower seller didn't qualify. He and Do-Hoppy were friends. Johnny, Angelo's son-in-law, didn't qualify because he'd only started work on the flower stall a few days before. But the Jervis commissionaire was the perfect candidate. Way across the road, behind a lay-by, dressed up in a campy uniform and cap . . .

"And when Do-Hoppy was telling me about it, he said he only saw the real joke of the thing when the bloke left him. He saw Murphy cross at the lights and go into the Jervis Hotel. So he watched, and saw him come back out in the commissionaire's uniform. Then it was his turn to see the joke, as he put it. Murphy must have been in a real panic. He decided to kill Do-Hoppy. But the old bloke had packed up and gone by the time he got off work. So he had to wait till the next morning."

She shook her head. "It's bizarre, Dan. They never actually met up just because Murphy always walked to work up the *other* side of Greeve Street. He told me that. Habit. But the habit was broken by the demolition of the place where he bought his breakfast every day. When he was talking to me it was obvious that the day before yesterday, at least, he was walking up Do-Hoppy's side. Once he started to do that it was just a matter of time before they met up at last. But, Dan, imagine . . . they worked on opposite sides of the same street for five and a half years and never really saw each other."

"Yeah . . ." Toby trudged on, shaking his head slowly, watching his feet. "Well, I did tell you at the start, Birdie. People in the city never look beyond their own noses. When you've been around as long as I have . . ."

"Poor old Do-Hoppy," said Birdie bitterly, ignoring him. "I hope they lock that bastard up and throw away the key."

"So does he," said Toby with a grim smile. "When his old mates find out he's alive they'll be very interested in a reunion. He doesn't reckon he'd enjoy that. That's why he confessed to the murder, once he knew we knew who he really was. He wants to be in maximum security."

"Oh, great! You mean we've helped him out."

"Ah, I wouldn't worry, Birdie," said Toby comfortably, steering her into the pub on the corner. "Trouble's in big, big trouble. They won't lose track of him again—in the nick or out of it. He'll be on the front pages again one fine day. Gangland revenge. Killer slain. Blood and guts. Police baffled. That sort of thing."

Birdie thought about that for a moment, then nodded. "Do-Hoppy's kind of headline!" she said. "He'd have liked that."

LADIES' DAY

"MEN ARE RESPONSIBLE for most violent crime, isn't that right? They kill more people. They have more serious car accidents, because they drink, and speed. Isn't that right? So how can you possibly say, Birdie, that women are just as aggressive. It plainly isn't true!" Kate banged her fist on the table in frustration. Froth spilled in a creamy wave over the side of her cup of coffee, and settled quietly into the saucer.

Verity Birdwood looked complacent. "No need to get excited, Kate. And don't shout. People are staring." She took a delicate sip of her own cappuccino. "I'm simply saying that aggression is in the eye of the beholder. There are different ways of expressing it. Even little ladies can kill. And just because most women don't fancy hitting people with blunt instruments or snipping off their toes with bolt cutters, that doesn't mean they're behind-hand in the aggression stakes. For heaven's sake—you've got a daughter. Surely you've seen it in her. And even if Zoe was a little paragon of mildness, which she isn't, I would have thought that school would have taught you all about female violence. My God, some of those girls were aggressive—all done with a smile, of course."

"Oh, bullshit." Kate stirred her coffee violently.

"And there are lots of ways of killing, you know," Birdie went on thoughtfully. "Ways even a proper little lady could think of. Stop stirring your coffee, Kate. It hasn't done anything to you. Now listen, I'm going to tell you a story. I never thought I'd tell it. Happened years ago. This is just between you and me. Okay?"

"Okay, of course. I won't tell a soul." Kate looked at her friend eagerly. This, at least, sounded interesting.

"Well, a few years ago, someone I knew quite well was going through a really bad time with her husband."

"Who? Do I know her?"

"Only slightly, I think. But I know her very well. I'll just call her Rose, for now anyway. It's the instance, not the person, that matters.

"Anyway, Rose was—is—an intelligent, attractive woman with a lot going for her. But at the time I'm talking about, she was going through a bit of a trough. She'd had a baby eighteen months before, and she'd left work to look after it. She was a bit over-weight, and a bit depressed. I think she was missing work, though she'd never admit it."

"She probably felt guilty about it," Kate nodded sagely. "Thought that if she was a good mother, she should love staying home with the baby all the time. Oh, God, I remember that. It's really—"

"Kate, do you want to hear the story or reminisce?" demanded Birdie sharply. "I have to be back at work at two-fifteen without fail. I swore."

"Okay, sorry. Go on."

"Right. Well, the thing was, Rose's husband—I'll call him Tim—had always been a real mate to her up till then. But gradually he started to get a bit tetchy. As he saw it, Rose was giving him a hard time. He'd get home after work and Rose would be droopy and tired, and doing the ironing or something, and wanting to get him fed quickly so she could buttonhole him about the trouble she'd had at the supermarket, and how the laundry tap needed fixing and the back door stuck and things like that, instead of sitting down with a drink and having a bit of a laugh and a chat, and a late, elegant little dinner like they used to do. He felt—"

"What about her?" Kate demanded passionately. "What about how she felt? She—"

"Kate, I'm not saying one was right and one was wrong," said Birdie quietly. "I'm just setting the scene as I saw it. I was seeing a lot of them at that time, and I could appreciate both sides— though Rose was my friend, not Tim, and it was her I felt sorry for. Anyway, after a while Rose started to complain that Tim was working too hard, staying at the office till all hours, even going in at the weekends, which hadn't been very typical of him up till then. I did wonder a bit, and then I started picking up little threads of gossip, you know how you do. There was this woman— a woman Tim and Rose both knew, and whom I'd met—who was making a real line for him. And he wasn't, according to what I heard, putting up much of a struggle."

"She was gorgeous with no kids, I suppose," sneered Kate. "Honestly, men are . . ."

"Got it in one. Free as a bird, she was, and as cool and collected, and organised and sophisticated as any silly man with a suddenly domesticated, unhappy wife could wish for."

"She sounds vile. What was her name?"

"Ah—how about Pamela? Does that sound cool enough? And you're right. She was quite vile, as far as women were concerned. They could see through her in a minute. Or at least, they could see that there wasn't anything *to* see. Men, apparently, felt differently."

Kate snorted.

"Anyway," Birdie went on, "Rose didn't say anything to me. Didn't say anything to anyone, as far as I know, but she suddenly stopped complaining about Tim working too hard, stopped talking about him at all, as a matter of fact. And she started looking jumpy, instead of depressed, and took up smoking again. So I knew . . ."

"She'd finally worked out what was happening."

"So it seemed." Birdie sipped her coffee thoughtfully. "I didn't know whether to be glad or sorry. I'd thought a dozen times of telling her myself, but I could never bring myself to do it. And anyway, I was sure it'd blow over. I thought Tim'd wake up. Pamela was just—just an image, that's all she was. No substance, no life, really. Just hair, and clothes and makeup, and cool and vanity. And Rose seemed so vulnerable, just then. I underestimated her, as it happened, but I really thought it would devastate her."

"Better that than have everyone feeling superior behind her back, I would have thought."

"No one was feeling superior, Kate. Would you have? Everyone was bloody angry."

"With the husband?"

"Oh, yes. But mainly with Pamela. She was a professional charmer. She could have had anyone—for a while, anyway. Why pick on a man with a wife and baby, that's what people thought."

"How sexist, to blame the woman! He knew what he was doing, didn't he?"

"In my view, in this case, the man was genuinely as much a victim as his wife. He was stupid, but it was as if he was just fascinated by Pamela. We'd seen it happen before, too. Pamela liked a challenge. She liked stealing attached men. Gave her a thrill."

Kate gazed at her silently for a minute. "All right. Go on," she said at last.

"Thank you. Anyway, one day Rose rang me and asked me to lunch at her place the following Friday. A nice, chatty lunch with the girls, it was going to be. It'd been ages since we all got together. Rose and me, Jan and Megan, Debbie—and Pamela. I asked her if she was sure about this, if she knew what she was doing, and she said yes, she did, and was I coming or not? So, of course, I said yes. I didn't want to encourage her in whatever bizarre madness she'd fallen into, but . . ."

"You couldn't resist it. Your curiosity was too much for you, wasn't it?" Kate smiled ruefully, and shook her head. "You're incorrigible!"

Birdie looked injured. "That wasn't it! Well, yes, I admit I was curious. But I wasn't sure what Rose was planning, but I thought she might . . . well . . . might need me, or something."

Kate regarded her thoughtfully. "You went for moral support, because she was your friend, and in trouble?"

Birdie shrugged.

"Not as tough as you pretend, are you?" Kate murmured.

Birdie shrugged again, irritably this time. "That's not the point. The point is, I had a bad feeling about the whole thing, and I made sure I got to Rose's place early on Friday, so I could see how the land lay, with no one else around. We were asked for twelve-thirty. I got there at twelve.

"Rose didn't seem any too pleased to see me so early, but I couldn't see why, because she was just about ready, as far as I could see, except for some last-minute cooking. She'd taken the baby to her mother's to give her a free hand, the house was tidy and the table was set, and she was all dressed up. She looked very nice, actually. I remember thinking that. But she was rather withdrawn, and intent, as if she was concentrating on something she wasn't going to talk about. I didn't like that a bit.

"She sat me down in the kitchen with a glass of wine, and

went on making the lunch. She was just finishing off this quiche, putting prawns and bits and pieces on top of it, and she chatted to me about this and that in this high, brittle sort of voice and I sat there wondering what on earth was really going on in her mind. Then she put the quiche in the oven, and made a salad, and got butter out of the fridge and so on and so on, chatting all the time and not saying anything. In fact, I know it sounds melodramatic, but I really got very nervous, sitting there. I kept looking at this big knife she was using to cut tomatoes. It was incredibly sharp— went through the tomatoes like butter. She caught me looking, and asked me what the matter was. Well, what could I say? I just stared at her and mumbled something or other, and she laughed and went on with what she was doing.

"I thought, how ridiculous I'm being. I'm actually suspecting Rose, of all people, of planning an act of violence. She's not that sort of woman. But when she went out to put the butter on the table, I nicked round and got the knife and put it out of sight at the back of one of the cupboards. Just in case. And I took these two cast-iron frying pans she'd cooked the prawns in out of the dishdrainer and hid them away too, in the pantry, because I thought they'd kill someone if they were thrown, especially the big one. And I also hid the skewers that were by the stove. And the carving knife and fork. I felt silly, but I did it.

"The doorbell rang and Megan and Debbie arrived. They'd worked with Rose, and they came in gossiping and laughing, and pleased to see her, and I started feeling better. I thought, well, maybe this genuinely is a get-together lunch. Maybe Rose doesn't know Tim's involved with Pamela, just that he's involved with someone. Maybe she's just trying to cheer herself up. Poor Rose. So I tried to be as pleasant as possible to Megan and Debbie, and they exerted themselves to be pleasant to me. I'd always thought they were a couple of prize twits, in fact, and they undoubtedly thought I was a prize weirdo, but we were all proper little ladies, all trying very hard, for Rose. By the time Jan, who was another old friend of Rose's, arrived we were all so full of bonfemie that we greeted her as though she was our long-lost sister. Jan, who was a different kettle of fish from Debbie and Megan, was looking very nervy, and kept looking at me and raising her eyebrows. I knew what she was trying to say. Was Pamela really coming? Did Rose *know?* If so, what on earth was going to happen?

"Anyway, twenty minutes late, as usual, Pamela arrived, a vision in cream, brown and gold, in an absolute gust of some suffocating scent, apologising and smiling and asking after the baby, and practically patting Rose on the head, she was so patronising. Rose was really quite impressive. She didn't flicker an eyelid. She was all charm. She admired Pamela's suit, and her blouse, and her shoes, and her hair, and asked her how work was, and all that. Then she looked at her watch and suggested we sit down and eat straightaway, since it was so late, and we all had to get back to work.

"She brought out a big tureen of soup, some sort of cold soup, it was, and served it, and it was quite delicious. But I can't say I enjoyed it. The atmosphere before Pamela's arrival had been a bit hysterical. Now it was ten times worse. Ladylike hysteria. Debbie and Megan had both drunk at least one glass of wine too many already, and were giggling with nerves and saying over and over again how lovely the food was, how lovely everything was. Jan was just shimmering with rage and kept smiling too much at Rose and looking daggers at Pamela. But Rose acted as if nothing was at all unusual, and Pamela, who loved above all things being the centre of intrigue and having people on the back foot, elegantly ate her soup, elegantly refused bread, and smiled like the Cheshire cat.

"Rose looked at her watch again, cleared away the soup plates, and brought out the salad and the quiche. She looked hard at me as she came in, and said she was sorry, but she was going to have to cut the quiche with a steak knife, because all her good knives had done the disappearing act. And everyone laughed and said oh, wasn't that always the way, and isn't it typical, and someone told about the times they had been stuck out camping with no tin opener and nothing but tinned food, and everyone wished they were anywhere but where they were, and that this dreadful meal would be over. Everyone but Rose and Pamela, apparently. They were having a great time. I'll remember it as long as I live.

"They kept on trying to get at one another. Like, while Rose was hacking away at the quiche, Pamela started going on about what a great little homebody Rose was, and what a lucky boy Tim was, all in that gushing way—'You're such a wonderful cook, Rosie. You're so *marvellous* at all that sort of homey thing. I wish I was, but I'm absolutely *hopeless.* I just *don't* have the patience. This dreary little lady used to try to teach us at school. It was all so *incredibly* boring, I couldn't stand it. And it's bored me stiff ever since. And, I mean, why bother, when you can always find some lovely man to take you out to dinner! Honestly, *honestly,* I can't boil an egg!'" Birdie flapped her hands and rolled her eyes in ludicrous imitation of the despised Pamela.

"And Rose—I remember at this point she'd finished hacking at the quiche and started walking round the table, offering it to people. Her hands were shaking so much she could hardly hold the plate. 'Oh, what a shame, Pamela,' she said, in this terrible, tight voice. 'Maybe if you enrolled in a class you might find you could learn, even now. I mean, it's not as though you're *that* old. And anyway I've never believed that stupid thing about new tricks and old dogs . . . or should that be old . . .'

"And then one or another of the other miserable lunchers— Debbie, I think—sort of half-screamed, half-giggled and said she was starving, and the thing was headed off. So Rose went on serving out until she got to Pamela and she stood there over her, with the little knife in her hand and this big empty platter with two vastly uneven, hacked-off pieces of quiche sliding round on it, and I had this terrible vision of Pamela with a steak knife in her neck or something, and I thought, oh, God, don't smile, Pamela. Don't say *anything*."

Kate laughed. "Birdie, you really are ridiculous sometimes. As if—"

"What? As if a little lady, a friend of mine, a nice, middle-class mother-of-one would really stick a knife in a rival? Well, maybe not. At least not in front of four rivetted witnesses. And as it happened, Pamela just slipped a piece of quiche off the plate without a word, and helped herself to salad, and the moment passed. But if looks could kill, Kate, Rose would have been a murderer then and there.

"Debbie and Megan and Jan chatted on and on, then. Through the quiche, and the salad, and the blueberries and cream, and several bottles of wine, and our first cup of coffee. The food was good, and everyone, including Rose and Pamela, ate every single thing on their plates, but I bet I wasn't the only one with indigestion. Rose kept glancing at her watch, and I stopped wondering why when I heard a key in the lock. It was Tim.

"Then I thought I understood. There was going to be a show-down. With witnesses. Rose had deliberately organised the lunch for a day Tim had planned to work at home in the afternoon. He must have expected us all to be there. If Rose hadn't told him, Pamela certainly would've. But as he had no idea Rose was onto the affair, he probably thought he and Pamela could just act breezy and friendly, and everything would be fine. A good chance, he might have thought, to disarm any future suspicion, if Rose should hear anything about the two of them in the future. Or maybe he just liked the idea of having his two women in the same room—the Boys' Own harem mentality. Who knows? And as for

Pamela, there was nothing she loved more than causing trouble, as long as she only had to sit and look elegant while it all happened around her.

"Anyway, the silly, self-conscious look Tim had on his face when he came in would have been a total giveaway, even if there had been a single soul there who didn't know what the situation was. The elaborately casual way he said hello to Pamela was excruciating to watch. He kissed everyone else—even me, and he's not all that fond of me—but he didn't kiss her. Just rested his fingers on her arm when he bent over to get some blueberries from the serving bowl. So casual, but with such concentration that he practically showed the whites of his eyes. And she smiled and everyone else boiled, because he was being so silly, and so obvious, and we were worried about Rose.

"But Rose smiled too, and offered him some coffee, and made him sit down. Pulled up a chair next to Pamela, and put him there, she did, smiling all the time. The others obviously thought she was being brave and defiant and all that, and you could feel the concentrated sympathy beaming out of them. The positive vibes, as Megan would have put it. But I knew her better than that. I'd known her for years. A person couldn't change that much in eighteen months. This diffident hausfrau thing was just a phase. She was up to something. I could feel it. And I was scared to death.

"It was only about ten minutes later that Pamela started looking seedy. She stopped laughing and talking and crossing and uncrossing her legs. She started looking rather white, and her eyes went dull. She put down her coffee, and asked for a glass of water. Tim jumped up and went and got her one, but she'd only had a few sips when she suddenly jumped up and rushed out of the room.

"She just made it to the bathroom, I'd say. Anyway, she didn't have time to shut the door, and we could all hear her being violently sick. Tim was very concerned, of course. Very startled, too. I don't suppose he'd ever thought of elegant Pamela in connection with basic functions before. Megan and Debbie and Jan pretended to be concerned, but they were all half-smiling, and obviously loving the whole thing. Rose was quite poker-faced. You couldn't tell what she was thinking. Pamela came back into the room as white as chalk under all that blusher and eye shadow that showed up like stripes on her skin. Her hair was limp and her lovely suit spotted with water where she'd had to wash it down. Rose was just so sweet to her. Put her in an armchair, offered black tea, a dry biscuit, a bed to lie down on.

"But Pamela brushed her away very snappily and lay back with her eyes closed. And then a minute later she rushed out again, and the whole thing was repeated, except this time she didn't make it to the bathroom. We could all hear her heaving and gasping in the hallway, and then running water in the bathroom and when she came back she looked even worse than before, and her shoes were all—well, unwearable would be the most delicate way to put it. She collapsed into the chair, and started crying and calling out for a doctor. She said she'd got food poisoning, and that she'd thought the quiche tasted odd, and that Rose had obviously used bad prawns and probably we'd all have to have our stomachs pumped. She was very sick and very white, and sweating, as petulant and mean-looking as hell.

"Rose said quietly that she was sorry, but if it was food poisoning, it was strange the rest of us were all right, since everyone was served from the same dishes. Pamela said she had a delicate constitution and therefore was probably feeling it first, and that furthermore Rose could bloody well pay for her shoes, which were Italian and had cost a fortune. And then she was sick again, in her lap.

"So then I said I thought she ought to go to hospital, and Rose agreed and asked Tim to take her. And Rose gave her a picnic rug to wrap herself in, because she was shivering, and a pair of old flat shoes to wear, and a bowl in case she was sick again, and helped her out to Tim's car. Tim was just about paralysed, but Rose found his keys and got him into the driver's seat, and told him to be sure and wait with Pamela in hospital to see she was all right, and off they went, with Pamela moaning and crying, huddled in her rug and clutching her bowl, and Tim showing the whites of his eyes again, but this time for a different reason.

"Rose went and cleaned up in the hall and under Pamela's chair, and then we had another cup of coffee, and we all talked about what on earth could have done the damage. No one was worrying about getting back to work on time by then. Rose was as cool as a cucumber, but I was worried sick. The others were taking it as a fortunate accident, but I knew it wasn't. Somehow or other Rose had given poison to Pamela. But how had she managed it? There wasn't one thing Pamela had eaten that we hadn't. Soup, salad, quiche, wine, blueberries and cream, all served from common dishes at the table. And coffee from a communal pot. Pamela didn't take sugar, so that was out. And what poison had Rose used? Was it one she could explain away somehow? Had she worked the whole thing out carefully? Or had she been so desperate that she just didn't care what happened when the contents of Pamela's stomach were analysed?

"It was a funny switch for me. Instead of trying to nail a murderer by working out how the deed was done, here I was desperately hoping a poisoner had covered her tracks well enough. And I couldn't ask her. I had to just sit there and drink coffee, and later on help do the dishes. Extra well. I insisted on that.

"So I was still there, trying to work out a way of asking her how she'd done it, and whether she'd been careful and so on, when Tim rang from the hospital. Pamela had had her stomach pumped. Food poisoning, they said. Mild salmonella. A bad prawn on the quiche she'd eaten. Pamela felt very seedy still. They said she was okay but she was demanding a second opinion. She was going to stay in hospital overnight, but he'd have to stay a bit longer because she was carrying on about having to share a room. She wanted a private one or nothing, and he'd have to try to straighten it out because the staff were getting irritated and Pamela wouldn't let up. Also, he'd have to go to her flat and get her a nightgown and other things, because she said she wouldn't sleep in the hospital gown because it was hideous, and couldn't wash her face with soap, and she didn't seem to have a single woman friend who could put a bag together for her and take it over. He didn't quite know what he should get. He thought she'd have hysterics if he missed anything. His car was a mess after the nightmare trip to hospital. He was exhausted. He didn't know when he'd be home. He kept thinking about when the baby was born, in that same hospital. They'd passed the maternity wing on their way in. A twelve-hour labour, and that terrible back pain. He'd remembered how brave Rose had been. Was she feeling okay? Whatever Pamela had said, she mustn't feel bad. It was just an accident. He would see her as soon as he could.

"Rose gave him a list of things she thought Pamela might want, and came back and told me all about it, and I could feel the relaxation in her flowing out all over the kitchen. She told me about it, and she laughed, just like she used to do in the old days. I laughed like a madwoman too, I was so relieved."

Kate drained her coffee and leant her chin on her hand, smiling wryly at her friend. "So, it was an accident after all, you panic-merchant," she said. "Why are you telling me all this, then? Where's your example of ladylike aggression? There was no murder. No one died, did they?"

Birdie grinned. "Depends on how you look at it," she said. "Something died, all right. Something was stone-cold dead after that afternoon."

"And what was that?"

"Tim's passion for Pamela, that's what. The neatest case of homicide I've ever seen. Rose didn't want to kill the *person.* I was mad to think she would. She just wanted to kill her husband's image of that person. And nothing brings out the true you better than an unpleasant illness, does it? Rose supplied the means by which Tim could see Pamela *in extremis.* And as she suspected, it wasn't a pretty sight."

"Sick as a dog," mused Kate dreamily. "Hard to be elegant wrapped in a picnic rug with a sick bowl on your knee and diarrhoea. And . . ."

"And even more important, screaming, complaining, carrying on even after you're better, and showing what a selfish egotistical little piece you are under all that charm. A clever plan—but ruthless, Kate, wouldn't you say? There's a ruthless streak in our Rose that I'd never thought was there. I've regarded her with new respect ever since."

"Have you now?" Kate smiled broadly, and shook her head. "But, Birdie, you're still talking as though the poisoning wasn't an accident. But it must have been. You said—"

"I said we all ate the quiche, and it was cut and served at the table. Not only that—we all helped ourselves from the plate. Even if Rose had done what I thought, and put somewhere on the quiche, carefully marked, a prawn that had been left out in the sun, or something, till it was safely off (and cooked, no doubt, by itself, in the smaller of the two pans I'd seen in the dishdrainer when I first arrived, while the others were cooked together in the big one) there was no way I could see that Pamela could be made to choose the piece with that prawn on it."

"Quite," laughed Kate. "So I really don't—"

"I only realised later how it was done. Because we're all such little ladies, we all took the next piece in the circle as it came to our turn. Pamela was last to be served and then there were two pieces left on the plate. One for her, and one for Rose. And at that point, I agree, she could have chosen either.

"So, it was a gamble on the poisoner's part, was it? Sounds unlikely to me." Kate shook her head.

"Highly unlikely. There was no gamble about it. Rose cut the quiche very roughly. I thought it was because she was upset. But no way. She offered that platter to Pamela with two very unevenly cut pieces of quiche on it and she knew, as well as she knew her own name, that Pamela would choose the smaller one. That's what ladies do, isn't it? And Pamela was *always* a lady—when things were going her way, anyway. Oh, yes. Ingenious. Unexpectedly ingenious."

Kate raised her eyebrows, and pushed back her chair.

"So have I won the argument, would you say?" Birdie teased.

"Maybe." Kate looked at her thoughtfully as they moved to the counter to pay. "Birdie, why haven't you ever said anything about this before? It's not like you to be so discreet."

"Oh, well." Birdie avoided looking at her by digging in the pocket of her jeans for money. "You know, the time was never right. And I didn't quite know whether I approved or disapproved, so I thought it was better not to say anything. But of course, Kate, you know I'd never talk about it to anyone else, don't you?"

"Oh, yes." Kate smiled to herself. "Best forgotten, isn't it? An unsavoury tale, Birdie. But . . . a pretty clever plan, wasn't it, all the same? And worked like a charm." She sighed. "But it's a shame about that quiche recipe. So good, but I've never cooked it since, you know. I just haven't felt like it. Funny, isn't it?"

Birdie looked at her as they moved out to the street, packed with lunchtime crowds. "Kate, sometimes you astound me."

"Good. Now about this '*unexpectedly* ingenious' business . . ."

And *that* argument went on for quite some time.

DEATH
IN STORE

KATE WATCHED HER DAUGHTER conversing with Santa Claus, and was conscious of a warm, teary glow. It was awfully pleasant. It had something to do with the lavishly decorated scene, so gratifyingly reminiscent of her own childhood memories of Christmas, something to do with the sound of carols and tiny bells lilting and tinkling enticingly over the muffled roar of shoppers in their annual buying frenzy, and a lot to do with the feeling that for once she was doing the right, the motherly, thing by Zoe.

Last year the visit to Santa had been a hurried, unsatisfactory affair at their local shopping mall. That Santa, whose rouged and sweating face was far too thin to fill out the woolly beard with which he'd been encumbered, had sat drooping on a metal chair twined with tinsel and plastic holly; the hapless creature of the Poppet Photo lady and an endless stream of mothers determined to make the photograph worth the wait.

Zoe had been quite happy with it all, having successfully delivered her modest requests and received the usual vaguely encouraging response plus a free balloon emblazoned with the name of the mall's major chain-store, and the photograph was nice, though Santa looked exhausted and Zoe rather stiff, but the experience had depressed Kate no end. Life was short, and childhood even shorter. Soon Zoe would have grown out of Santa and all his works—the power and magic of that particular myth would disappear from her life like so many others. Next year, Kate had sworn, they'd do it properly. Go to the city. To Fredericks', the big store where her mother had always taken her at Christmas; the store whose Christmas decorations were famous, whose long-serving Santa had been written up in the paper several times, where things were done with grace and dignity and style, in the old-fashioned way.

Watching Zoe whispering shyly to the kind, jolly figure in red on his sumptuous golden throne, Kate could almost remember perching on Santa's knee in just this spot, new white sandals swinging off the floor, little straw handbag clutched in one small, sweaty hand. It had been magical. It must be magical now, for Zoe, though she wasn't the white-sandal-and-little-straw-handbag type, if any little girls now were. Discreetly, a red-and-white-clad young woman moved forward and her camera flashed, capturing the moment, not two fixed and nervous smiles. Kate sighed with satisfaction. Well worth the money. Well worth it. Now Santa was reaching down into the sack beside his throne. It was filled with brightly wrapped little packages tied with gold ribbon. No freebie promotional balloons for Santa's visitors at Fredericks'. A special gift for every child to take home and put under the tree. That was the Fredericks' tradition. Zoe accepted her red-wrapped gift gravely, and slipped down from Santa's knee. Head down, she self-consciously made her way over to her mother.

"Well, how was that?" Kate, filled with maternal pride, bent down to greet her.

"Good," murmured Zoe, very aware of smiling onlookers.

"Can we have lunch now? You said we were meeting Birdie. Let's go." She tugged at her mother's hand, willing her to stand upright and behave.

"What did Santa say?" persisted Kate, as they made their way through the forest of Christmas trees that surrounded Santa's Grotto (as Fredericks' had dubbed it) to the escalator. "Was he nice?"

"Yes, but he's not the real Santa, you know, Mum," explained Zoe gently. "He's a Santa's helper. Like the one we saw last year at the mall. The sweaty one. He was nice too. They're mostly nice."

"Oh. Yes, well . . ."

"But this one was *very* nice," nodded Zoe hastily and reassuringly. "He talked much more than they usually do, and he gave me a present to take home—a red one, that's special, because most of them were green and blue—and guess what, Mum, he said I *could* have a bike!"

"What!"

"Yes, he did. He said what did I want most really and truly, and I said a bike, and he said okay!" Zoe's eyes were shining at the memory.

"But Zoe, Daddy and I have told you that—"

"I know, but he said Santa could do it. So you and Dad don't have to. See? And he said he'd bring a Barbie and a black T-shirt with a skull on it, too. *And* a surprise, which is what I said I wanted first, like you said." Zoe nodded thoughtfully. "It was a good idea to come here, Mum. You were right."

Kate was lost for words.

The cafeteria was crowded with women slumped exhausted in chairs surrounded by bulging plastic bags, and children drinking milkshakes while jealously guarding their own special parcels which often included a little package, the gorgeously gold-beribboned trophy of their visit to the Fredericks' Santa. Kate winced as she looked at them. The simple tackiness of last year's experience was starting to seem rather appealing. She watched Zoe crouch down to watch a Christmas video discreetly playing under a glowing tree in one corner of the room, and sighed.

"What's wrong with you?" her friend Verity Birdwood asked sourly. "You're supposed to love all this sort of thing."

"Oh, well, I do," said Kate defensively. "I'm just a bit . . ." Then she rallied. It didn't do to let Birdie get the advantage. "Anyway, have you had a lovely morning, Birdie? Absorbing the festive atmosphere and all? A wonderful, warm Christmas piece coming up?" Much amused, Kate sniggered at her friend's pained expression. She was the last person anyone sensible would send to research a TV program about Christmas in a big store. Everyone else must be on holidays.

Verity Birdwood curled her lip and stirred her coffee. "It wouldn't be so bad if they wanted a piece on human folly," she muttered. "There's plenty of material for that. I've never seen anything like it. Like lemmings, they all are. The money! The plastic, I should say. You can smell it. Hot plastic. Click, click, fifty dollars, sixty dollars, a hundred dollars. Spending like there's no tomorrow, the lot of them. Ludicrous. The staff are run off their feet and cranky as blazes, the shoplifters are out in force, taking everything they can lay their hands on, the management's on tenterhooks because Christmas makes or breaks the place . . . there's a story here all right, but those idiots don't want it. They want some drivelling piece all tidings of comfort and joy. It's sickening."

"Oh, bah, humbug to you too. Why on earth did they send you to do this, Birdie?"

"Everyone else's on holidays."

"Well, look, can't you just relax and enjoy it? There's lots more to it than you're seeing. Have you been up to the toy floor?" urged Kate. "The decorations, the Santa? The kids up there are just—"

Birdie rolled her eyes. "I got taken up there first thing this morning to meet the man in person, and see the kids lining up. Do you know there were women in the queue with babies that couldn't even sit up? And little toddlers with dummies in their mouths who screamed just at the thought of sitting on this crazy man's knee? And teenagers who looked as if they'd break his kneecap if they tried to. Madness! But every year it's the same, apparently. The Fredericks' Santa's some kind of national treasure. Part of the great tradition—and he knows it, too. His name's Ben Bluff, if you'll believe it, and I think he thinks he *is* Santa Claus. Dimpled, chuckling old sod. But he earns his keep, I'll say that. What a job! Kids, kids, kids from nine to five, six days a week. Fifteen-minute tea-break morning and afternoon, and an hour for lunch. What a nightmare! I get to talk to him between one-thirty and two. I'll ask him how he stands it, and how come he's so wise and wonderful."

"I don't know about wise and wonderful. High-handed, more like it," said Kate, her resentment winning out over her self-appointed role as Yuletide champion. "He promised Zoe a bike. Santas aren't supposed to do that sort of thing."

"I thought that's just what they were supposed to do."

"No, no. They're supposed to sort of go 'Ho, ho, well, we'll see, my little friend,' and things like that. I mean, how did he know we could afford a bike? Or wanted Zoe to have one, which we don't, in fact. Or anything? It was dreadful. The skinny old bloke at the mall last year was better value from that point of view. At least he kept to the 'Ho, ho, we'll see' rules."

Birdie grinned. "Oh, well, you've only got yourself to

blame." She glanced at her watch. "I'd better go soon, Kate. I've got to meet my little window-dressing friend in the Toy Department in ten minutes."

Russell Dijohn, presently absorbing a light lunch at his desk on the deserted tenth floor and checking over his messages (please ring your sister Marie, please ring Mr. Simms of Jewellery, please ring Mr. Silvester of Toys, Mrs. Stack of Lingerie rang, your sister rang again, your dry-cleaning is ready—all that could wait) would have bridled to hear himself described in such terms. He took himself and his responsibilities rather seriously these days. However he had begun at Fredericks', he was now a man of substance in the pecking order, totally in charge of store decoration and reporting directly to the General Manager. His budget was huge, his staff large (though never large enough, of course), his studio-office spacious, well-lit and provided with a pleasant view. He had the run of the store and, especially at this vital time of year, his orders and machinations regarding the placement of ornaments on the floor and display of goods to augment them, combined with strong personal supervision and an almost fanatical attention to detail, caused confusion, frustration and occasional fury among the harried department heads and their staff.

Russell was aware of their resentment but, with a flick of his straight, dark forelock, sublimely rose above it, reasoning that more pedestrian minds could not be expected to sympathise with Art. Today, as he mechanically initialled expense sheets and nibbled the smoked salmon on black bread his secretary had prepared for him before going out for her own cheese on toast, he was aware that over their own lunch some of his adversaries would again be comparing notes and complaining to each other about him. But that worried him not at all. They could complain all they liked, silly old windbags. He knew management was behind him in his endeavours, seeing them, quite rightly in Russell's opinion, as vital to the creation of the Fredericks' Christmas ambience. And the opportunities and satisfactions of his present position were so extremely valuable to him that the grumblings of a few old men and women were unlikely to be more than a momentary irritation.

Russell smiled to himself, and flicked the folder closed. Everything was going smoothly, and he was looking forward to the rest of the afternoon. The little Birdwood woman was very dreary, but he never tired of showing off his handiwork to interested parties, and Ben Bluff was always impressive. Hopefully he'd be on form for the interview.

For the first time, a tiny cloud of concern crossed Russell's face. Come to think of it, Ben had seemed a bit off-colour first thing this morning. A bit nervy. Difficult, even. He'd wanted to talk, and Russell had meant to pop down to see him again before lunch. He'd wanted to check out the Christmas tree lights, anyway, and put some extra presents in Santa's sack, which should always look excitingly full. How irritating that in his preoccupation with Verity Birdwood's tour he had forgotten. If Ben got sick or dropped his bundle, that would ruin everything. He was the centrepiece of the whole Christmas shebang. Had been for years. He was vital.

Russell sighed. He was overreacting. Stress was making him get things out of proportion. Ben must have had some upset over the weekend. Or maybe that floorwalker in Toys—Ernie Simpson, or whatever his silly name was—had been needling him again. There was no doubt that Ben was getting to be a bit of a prima donna these days, needing lots of tender loving care and the star treatment and so on. Annoying, but probably inevitable, given the attention paid to him, an attention that Russell had been keen to foster. He was without doubt the perfect Santa Claus and Verity Birdwood would be charmed by him. As of course she must be by the whole setup, though the poor thing was too shy and nervous to say much. No one could fail to be impressed by the decorations this year, for example. In Russell's view they were his best yet. And the organisation! Of course, some of its most brilliant aspects weren't for public consumption, which was almost a shame, so neat were they. But the magic must be at the forefront, the sleight of hand concealed. That was the essence of his genius. Russell took a sip of lime juice and leaned back in his comfortable chair. Yes, he had undoubtedly made a big success of this. He was Fredericks' most valuable asset, and they knew it. It cost them, of course, he mused, brushing a small thread of tinsel from the cuff of his elegant, very expensive jacket. But he was worth every penny.

"He's drunk with power, of course," growled Simms of Fine Jewellery and Watches, eyeing a large dill pickle on his plate and wondering if he should risk it. "I mean, a bit of decoration's one thing, but you've seen what he's done. All the jewellery on that tree, and in the angels' hair and everything? It's madness! I mean, for one thing, that's totally the wrong way to display gems, isn't it? And the security risk! Worse than even that treasure chest idea last year. And heaven knows we lost a bit then. I said to him, I'm not taking the responsibility. I wash my hands of it. No way of telling what we've got and haven't got now. For all I know there's someone pocketing something every ten minutes. It's beyond me why John Fredericks has given him his head like he has."

"Poor young John isn't the man his father was," pronounced the redoubtable Una Stack of Lingerie and Corsetry. She had been at Fredericks' for thirty years, and was a perfectly structured advertisement for the more rigid examples of her own wares. "He was on the floor only yesterday and I tackled him. I was moderate, and I was tactful. I said the angels in the nightwear were fine. Very pretty, I said, actually, lying through my teeth, since sick-making is closer to the mark in my view. And it's almost sacrilegious, isn't it? Putting sheer nights and negligees on angels?

"But there are just too many of them, John, I said. We sell more than nightwear, I said, and I've got all the bras and corsetry lines stuck away in this crowded little corner, it's so infuriating. And you know what he said? He asked me what sells the best in my department at Christmas. So I said nightwear, of course, by a long way. And then he just shrugged and smiled at me, said, 'Well, that's your answer, isn't it?' and strolled off. Now, I ask you!" She looked triumphantly around the table. Everyone nodded sagely. Frank Silvester of Toys raised his grey head and blinked around like an ancient tortoise. "No one," he droned, "has any conception . . ." The voice faded.

A respectful silence fell. Everyone present conceded that whatever their own troubles, they were as nothing compared to those of Silvester of Toys.

"Did you do the measurements, Frank?" asked kind Popescue of Bedding encouragingly.

The grey man nodded slowly. "Thirty-seven per cent," he said, and set his thin lips. "Thir-ty-sev-en per cent of my floor space he's taken this year."

"No!" exclaimed Mrs. Stack.

Silvester nodded again. "Yes. Hard to credit, isn't it? But it's the truth, as I sit here. Fifteen per cent more than last year, twenty-five more than the year before, thirty-two more than—"

"They've extended Santa's Grotto, haven't they?" Mrs. Stack had known Frank for a long time, and had learned to be ruthless.

"Ah, yes," sighed Silvester. "They've extended it. They've put a forest in front of it, and a dressing room behind it, and the Lord knows what else. And Ben Bluff sits up there like Lord

Muck, right in the middle of the board games section, as should be, driving Ernie Simpson half-wild with his carry-on and giving away presents to all comers, no questions asked. So why do they need to buy anything, eh? Not that you can see any of the stock, it's that packed and stuffed into what's left of the floor."

"Yes, well, Mr. Russell Dijohn's riding for a fall, if you ask me," said Simms confidently. "It's the tail wagging the dog. You've got to display the goods, haven't you? Or where are your sales?"

"Yours are down on last year, are they, Vernon?" Mrs. Stack pounced hopefully.

He hesitated. "Well, not exactly down, no," he said at last. "They were up last week. Up considerably." Then he rallied. "But it was a freakish sort of figure. Bound to drop through the floor this week."

Mrs. Stack stirred her tea. "Mine were up too," she volunteered, looking at no one. "Frank?"

"Up," growled the tortoise joylessly. "But I maintain—"

"Petru?"

"Up," said Popescue of Bedding gloomily.

"George?"

George Brown of Books and Stationery was a man of few words. He swallowed the last of his coffee and pointed meaningfully towards the ceiling.

A heavy depression settled over the group.

"Oh, bum," said Mrs. Stack.

"And that's all there is to it, love." Ben Bluff twinkled benignly at Birdie, and drained the last of his tea from a thick, white mug with Merry Christmas written on it in gold. "I'm an ordinary old bloke who has nothing to do but sit on his arse waiting for the pension cheque to come most of the year, and who loves kiddies. I look forward to Christmas at Fredericks' like I was a kiddie myself."

"And you don't ever get sick of the children? I mean, the noise, and the . . . mess and everything?" asked Birdie, wincing slightly at the memory of the sticky-fingered, overexcited queue waiting at the edge of Russell's "magic forest" for Santa's reappearance.

Ben Bluff guffawed. It was almost a genuine "Ho, ho, ho." Any minute, Birdie thought, he'll be laying his finger on the side of his nose or suggesting she sit on his knee. She was no bigger than some of those girls in the queue, after all. "Oh, no, I never get sick of them, love. And they're most of them good as gold when they get into the grotto, you know. Like little mice. And as for mess, well, that comes with the job, doesn't it? Bubble gum in the beard, chocolate on the pants, baby dribble all over the place. That's why there's spare suits and beards in here." He waved his hand around his compact little dressing room. Then he leaned forward, twinkling slyly at her. "And I've had worse than chocolate all over me too," he murmured. "Some of the little ones, they've waited a long time to get to me, you understand, and . . ." He paused delicately, and then hooted with laughter at Birdie's shocked face.

"You should see yourself," he gasped. "I knew that'd get to you. Ah, I can see you haven't had much to do with kids. But I've got seven grandchildren, and nothing worries me. They come round to my place for a swim in the pool or a game of tennis or whatever, like they did yesterday, and their parents can't do a thing with them. But I can." He paused for a moment, and gradually all the laugh lines dropped away from his face, leaving it sober and intent.

He leaned forward and his voice grew husky. "I understand

them, see. I talk their language. I'm straight with them. I don't make promises I can't keep. And I love them. That's what makes me a good grandpop, and that's what makes a good Santa. That's what a lot of these people at Fredericks' don't understand. There's this floorwalker here, Ernie Simpson, for example. He used to play Santa himself here, years ago. He's got no respect for me. None at all. Thinks I bung it on. I know. But little kids, you know —little kids—they haven't been mucked up by the world like we have, not yet. They can smell a hypocrite. Oh, you'll fool them for a while maybe, but in the end they'll twig."

He nodded slowly. "They'll twig, and then you're done like a dinner, as far as they're concerned. You've lost them, and they've lost something they'll never get back. Innocence, I suppose you'd call it."

Birdie was still thinking about that when she noticed Russell Dijohn hovering at the doorway. "I think we'll have to leave it there, Verity," he murmured, "so Ben can get back to work." He cast a professional eye over Ben Bluff, trotted over to him and tweaked at a little bit of beard straying out to the side.

The misty-eyed philosopher disappeared and a cranky old man took his place. Bluff batted his hand away impatiently. "Aw, leave it alone, will you?" he growled. "And I need to talk to you, Russell. You never came back this morning. Left me here like a shag on a rock with a blinding headache. I had a shocking night, too, so what do you expect?"

Russell looked harried. "Okay, Ben, okay. Having a few problems, are you? Look, I'm sorry about that. Just hold on, mate, all right? I'll speak to Silvester, and to Ernie Simpson if necessary. I'll fix it. I'll be back before the end of the day, and I'll catch up with you then. Promise. Okay?" His eyes slid swiftly sideways to the watching Birdie and back again. Ben Bluff shrugged sulkily.

"I'll send my girl down with some pills for you, Ben," Russell coaxed.

"Don't need any now," growled the old man perversely. "That gink Simpson gave me some of his, and the break did me good, I must say. Had a bit of a lie-down. Headache's gone now. But . . ."

Russell nodded enthusiastically. "Great," he said heartily. "Well, Ben, I'll take Verity off now, and catch up with you later. It's just on two, and you've got some very anxious kids out there." He gestured at the curtained doorway leading to the magic forest.

Ben looked at him sourly, brushed some crumbs from his knee, stood up and slung his sack over one shoulder. Then he turned to Birdie. "Good-bye, little lady," he said, nodding benignly at her. "May your troubles be little ones. And a Merry Christmas to you."

"And to you," said Birdie, a bit taken aback. She watched as the red-caped figure crossed the tiny room, pushed a button on the cassette player standing there and pulled the curtain back with a flourish. Then, as the sound of "Jingle Bells" filled the air, Ben Bluff threw back his shoulders, hitched his less-than-bulging sack more firmly on his back, and, smiling, went out to meet his public.

"Could I have a word, Russell?" Frank Silvester blinked at them in the dim light of the passage that led from Santa's little haven to the staff amenities room. He had obviously been hovering in wait for some time. Russell Dijohn winced in annoyance.

"It's a bit awkward at the moment, Frank," he said. "Could you—?"

"Look, I'll be all right for a few minutes, Russell," said Birdie, seizing her opportunity to be alone for a moment. Russell was not restful company. "I'll wait for you outside. Watch Ben at work, talk to some of the children and so on. Good material." She slipped quickly away, past the melancholy figure of Silvester of Toys, before Russell could object. Silvester's droning voice followed her through the doorway. ". . . Won't stand for it anymore," he was saying. "I won't stand for it . . . measured this morning . . . thirty-seven per cent . . . past a joke. And if you and Ben Bluff think you can just come in and . . ."

Birdie raised her eyebrows. Trouble in elfland. She would have loved to hear more, but Russell Dijohn was already craning his neck past Silvester's bowed shoulder, to check that she had gone. She passed into the cooler, fresher air of the store proper, and wandered back to the entrance to Santa's Grotto.

A trail of mothers and children wound through the forest of Christmas trees that surrounded the grotto on all sides. Carols played faintly, and the children chattered excitedly as the line moved slowly forward and they caught tantalising glimpses of the great man himself, seated on a golden throne in the frosted, dimly lit cave, with his sack of presents beside him. Wisps of gold and white gauze hung at the grotto entrance, stirring gently in the same breeze that set the hundreds of tiny silver bells on the Christmas trees ringing and moved the tinkling crystal icicle mobiles in the grotto. It was certainly impressive, and even Birdie, who had met Ben Bluff in the flesh, who had seen the dozens of cunningly placed fans that whirred away all day to create this effect, found herself strangely moved by the atmosphere. So absorbed was she, in fact, that she quite failed to see the figure that loomed up before her as she stepped out of the forest.

"Beg your pardon, madam," said the impeccably-dressed floorwalker, discreetly removing his foot from under hers. "Can I help you?"

"Oh, my fault. Sorry." Birdie looked up at him. "No, no, I'm fine, thanks. Just watching your Santa Claus. He's quite amazing, isn't he?"

"Oh, yes," murmured the man politely, and his eyes took on a glazed look. Birdie glanced at the neat name tag on his buttoned-down chest. E. Simpson. Ah, this must be the Ernie Simp-

son who was giving Ben Bluff trouble. He looked mild-mannered
enough, and yet there was something . . .

"It's such a difficult job," she began experimentally, and to
her satisfaction the fish rose quickly to the bait.

"Oh, I wouldn't say that," said Ernie Simpson rather loudly,
staring over her head. "Some people make a great song and dance
about it, certainly, but as I've said to management time and again,
anyone with a genuine affection for children could do it. I, for
example, have—" He broke off suddenly, and a dull red flush
crept over his face as he rather belatedly realised the inappropri-
ateness of his response under the circumstances.

"Some people do get a bit self-important, don't they?" said
Birdie innocently, as though she'd noticed nothing. "Especially
when they've had a bit of publicity, like your Santa. It must be
awfully irritating for you all." She waited hopefully.

But Ernest Simpson, loyal Fredericks' employee for over
twenty years, wasn't going to be drawn again into indiscretion. He
murmured something noncommittal and moved aside to let her
pass. With regret Birdie left him, but once she was far enough
away to escape his attention, she turned back. He was standing
where she'd left him, his eyes fixed on the red figure in the grotto.
His fists were clenched, his whole body rigid, his mouth set into a
tight, grim line. He didn't look so mild-mannered now. In fact, if
looks could kill . . .

Russell found Verity Birdwood an energetic tourist that afternoon.
And if she seemed a little more interested in Ben Bluff and the
store decorations than even he had expected, that was all to the
good. It was unfortunate that in her enthusiasm she mentioned
the old man and praised Russell's work to practically every staff
member she met, because some of them greeted her effusions

with barely concealed ill humour. That old bitch Una Stack in Lingerie, for example, had sneered almost openly, and Simms in Jewellery and Watches had favoured them with a totally inappropriate harangue on store security. But luckily Russell had been able to gloss over any unpleasantness, and the little researcher had seemed quite oblivious to it, anyway. She was obviously having a marvellous time, and as they moved from department to department through the afternoon, her eyes developed quite a sparkle behind her thick glasses.

Russell said good-bye to his charge at five-thirty and made his way back to his office with a sense of relief. The PR value of this program would be great, and he had wanted to do the guided tour himself. He, after all, would be the main talent in the planned feature and, with his usual attention to detail, he wanted to make sure it all went well from the beginning. But still, there were so many demands on his time, and he'd been occupied with her for the whole day, barring lunch. Now he'd have to try to catch up.

He stepped out of the lift and walked towards his studio, marshalling his thoughts. He'd work late—later than usual, anyway, for he was rarely out of the building before seven. He'd leave the full tour of the floors to check the decorations for once. After all, he'd been round the whole place once already today. He could come in early tomorrow to do that, and fill up Santa's sack, and . . . He stopped dead and clicked his teeth impatiently. Oh, for goodness' sake, he'd forgotten Ben Bluff! Again! The old boy would be furious.

He half-turned to go back to the lift, glanced at his watch, and hissed in annoyance. It was just too late. They'd be packing up down in Toys now, and he had masses of work to do anyway. He'd never got back to Simms or Mrs. Stack either. They'd be fuming. Well, too bad. But he really had to ring Marie. That sister of his was getting to be a real nuisance, but she'd rung twice and she'd give him hell if he didn't call. Ben would have to wait till morning. After all, what could be so important that one night could make a scrap of difference?

The rain was pelting down on Tuesday morning. At eight o'clock it was as dark as it had been before dawn. Esme Stack and her mother arrived dripping at Fredericks' discreet staff entrance, shook out their umbrellas, and said good-bye for the day. Clammy in her plastic raincoat, Esme slowly made her way upstairs to the Toy Department. She thought almost with wonder of the state of mind in which she'd made the same trek only two weeks ago. She'd been so glad to get the Santa's helper job originally—she needed the money, that was for sure. But after two weeks of watching Ben Bluff fascinating ankle-biters, nursing swaddled, unconscious bundles and dealing with gum-chewing teenagers all of whom looked exactly the same, her enthusiasm had dwindled to nothing, and a numb resentment had taken its place.

She'd set up her little photographic studio with such hope six months ago. She'd had the cards printed, put the ads in the paper, slaved over the prints to be sent to magazines, book publishers and galleries, and waited for the world to take an interest. And had the world responded? Not by the flicker of an eyebrow. The only job she'd been offered in two months was this one: dressing up in silly clothes and taking happy snaps of overawed kids. And even that her mother had organised for her. It was ironic, how things turned out.

Her feet dragged as she stepped off the escalator and made her way towards Santa's Grotto and the staff amenities room, pulling off her raincoat as she went. She noticed what she was doing and deliberately speeded up. She didn't want any of those busybodies up here noticing her reluctance and commenting on it afterwards.

"Esme!" The hoarse whisper penetrated her consciousness like a voice in a dream. She looked around and saw no one. There was no one on the floor at all. That would be right. Mum was always early. She lived and breathed bloody Fredericks', as if Fredericks' cared. She got no thanks for her devotion, as far as her daughter could see.

"Esme, here! Esme!" There it was again. She glanced round again, and then out of the corner of her eye caught a movement among the Christmas trees ahead of her. Russell Dijohn was there, hanging onto the curtain that masked the entrance to the staff-only section of the floor. Her stomach lurched. He looked strained and grim. Quite unlike his normal, ostentatiously busy, arrogant little self. As she reached him he let go of the curtain and took hold of her arm instead.

"There's no one else here, Esme. You'll have to help me. You'll have to be calm."

"I am calm," she said pointedly, her mother's daughter. "What's the matter?"

"I want you to go and stand outside Ben's—the Santa's— changing room, just for a minute, while I go and do something. I want you to stand there and not let anyone in. All right? And not go in yourself. Or look in. Can you do that for me?"

"But what's the matter? Is Ben sick or something? He had an awful headache yesterday, you know. He shouldn't have been at work." She stared at his pale face insolently.

"Just do it, Esme, all right?" snapped Russell. "Please!"

She shrugged and wandered down the narrow corridor, finally taking up a mock sentry pose with her back to the curtain screening off Ben's area. He nodded at her, raised a warning finger, and darted away. Esme looked down at her folded arms, and slowly unfolded them. Deliberately she turned and tweaked back the curtain.

Ben Bluff, red-caped, black-booted, lay face down on the

floor of the little room, like a huge, abandoned toy. And from his back, to complete the illusion, protruded what looked like a silver key. The rain beat against the window. His colour has run, thought Esme, stupidly. It's run all over the floor. Her fingers tightened on the rough fabric.

"Good morning!" the voice reached her from somewhere very faraway, it seemed to her. She turned slowly, blinking, and a shape moved in the dimness of the little corridor. For a moment Esme panicked. She screamed and tugged at the curtain convulsively, pulling it partly off its track.

"Is something the matter, dear?" Ernie Simpson, solid and comforting in a rain-spattered all-weather coat came closer, his mild face enquiring and solicitous.

Esme found herself trembling and unable to speak. She had always been able to hide her emotions. She'd always been able to trust in her sangfroid. But not this time. She pointed wordlessly and watched, fascinated, as Simpson moved through the doorway. She saw him stumble, and begin to fall, his arms waving wildly, his eyes wide with horror. She saw him roll helplessly against the dead thing on the floor, his hands puddling in sticky scarlet blood, his knees crushing the carton that had been his downfall, the dozens of gold-ribboned Santa gifts tumbling green and blue around his big, wet, black shoes. Then she screamed, and this time she couldn't stop.

"It's a disaster for us, that's all. An absolute disaster." Russell gnawed at his lip, his brow furrowed ferociously.

Detective Sergeant Dan Toby hitched at his belt and nodded at the exquisite young man before him. "I can see that," he said blandly. "Having your Father Christmas done to death with a pair of scissors. Pretty disastrous. Not very festive. Not too good for the man in question, either."

Russell looked uncomfortable. "Oh, of course, I'm sorry. It's not that I'm callous. I know I must sound it. It's just . . ."

"I understand, Mr. Dijohn." Toby turned away. Shallow little twerp, he thought, disgusted with Russell for simply existing and with himself for playing smart-arse games. He met the disapproving gaze of Detective Constable Milson, coolly taking notes on thin, crossed knees in a corner of the room, and restrained an impulse to bare his teeth. Why they kept lumbering him with cold-fish Milson was beyond his comprehension. They knew he couldn't stand the man—God knows he'd told them often enough. They were probably all too aware the feeling was mutual, in fact.

Toby tried to pull himself together. "You said, Mr. Dijohn, that Ben Bluff seemed a bit seedy yesterday. That right?"

Russell almost curled his lip, then appeared to think better of it. "He seemed not to be in his normal good health and spirits," he said prissily. "He said he had a headache, and hadn't slept well the night before. He wanted to talk something over with me."

"And what was that?"

Russell winced. "I don't know," he said. "I was very busy yesterday, as it happened. I had someone with me when I saw him in the morning, and I didn't manage to get back to him all day."

"Ah." Toby leaned back in his chair. "But didn't I understand from the unfortunate floorwalker who fell on the body, Mr. . . . ah . . ."

"Ernest Simpson, sir," droned Milson from his corner.

"Thank you, Milson," snapped Toby irritably. "Yes, Mr. Simpson. Didn't I understand from him that you visited Toys three times yesterday?"

Russell looked very irritated himself. "As Mr. Simpson very well knows, I visited Toys once for literally two minutes before the store opened, to refill Santa's sack. I do this every day, but yesterday morning I was in a tearing rush. The other times were in the company of an ABC researcher, Verity Birdwood, who was with me all day yesterday. I had no opportunity whatsoever to exchange more than a few words with Ben Bluff alone." He noticed Toby's expression and paused. "Anything wrong?" he snapped.

"Oh, no, no." Toby refrained from looking at Milson again, but could feel a cold glower trained at the back of his neck. He rubbed it thoughtfully. "I've bumped into Verity Birdwood once or twice before, that's all. Coincidence." He forced himself to smile at Russell in what he hoped was a reassuring manner. "So, you didn't see Ben Bluff, to talk to properly that is, at all yesterday. Is that why you came to see him first thing this morning?"

Russell hesitated. "Well, as I said, I usually do—did—see him then, anyway. He always got in early, to dress, and of course at this time of year I always get in early too, so I'd come down to see him while there was no one else around in Toys."

"Why did you do that, Mr. Dijohn?" Toby spoke quietly, but Russell looked startled.

"Well, um . . . I just did. It was a habit I'd got into, I suppose. He's—he was—the centrepiece of my work here, if you see what I mean. I liked to make sure he was okay, and looked okay, and the grotto had been cleaned properly and so on. And I'd bring a fresh supply of presents for the sack. He liked me to come first thing, too, for a personal chat, if you see what I mean."

"Made him feel important, you mean?"

"Yes, I suppose so. But in fact he *was* important. And it didn't hurt me to, well, indulge him, did it? Especially when . . ." Russell boggled slightly and his voice trailed off.

"Yes, Mr. Dijohn?"

"Well, nothing, really." Russell laughed self-consciously and cleared his throat. "Sorry, I'm not feeling quite myself. Don't quite know what I was going to say."

Toby let it ride. "Anyhow, Mr. Dijohn, you were the first to see him this morning, as usual, were you?" he asked mildly. "You know I was!" Russell was very rattled. Toby saw with satisfaction that his forehead gleamed slightly with sweat. The impeccably knotted tie, too, had been fidgeted a trifle to one side. There was a pause, and then Russell's jaw dropped slightly and his eyes widened. "Except," he squeaked, "for the person who killed him, of course. I mean, I was the first person to see him *dead*. You don't think . . ."

"Oh, I don't think anything, Mr. Dijohn. I'm just getting the picture, that's all. Lots of people to talk to yet." Toby flicked open a tiny notebook, licked a blunt finger and turned a page or two. "Mrs. Boynton, our late Santa's daughter; Mr. Silvester, head of Toy Department; Esme Stack, the little photographer girl—"

"Santa's helper," amended Russell automatically.

"Yes . . ." Toby solemnly made a note. "Wears a little red skirt, does she?" he asked hopefully. "And fishnet stockings?"

"Not fishnet stockings," protested Russell, shocked. "White tights. And red boots. And a white fur hat."

"Very tasteful. She was in early too, I gather. Another dedicated Fredericks' worker?"

"Not exactly." Russell had recovered some of his composure. "Esme is usually early, but that's because she comes to work with her mother, who has been head of our Lingerie Department for many years."

"Ah—nepotism!" Toby leaned back and grinned broadly. "Jobs for the daughters, eh?"

"She's only a casual, Mr. Toby," said Russell stiffly. "And a good professional photographer."

"Oh, of course. And did she and Santa get on, Mr. Dijohn? Did she enjoy being en-grottoed with him day in, day out?"

"I'm afraid I really don't know." Russell looked at his watch and stood up. "Have we finished, do you feel, Mr. Toby? I'm going to be frantically busy this morning, and really—"

"Oh, sure, we're finished for now." Toby smiled benignly up at him. "We'll have a little chat later, maybe, when you're feeling more yourself. And you can have your grotto back tomorrow, I'd say. What on earth will you do in the meantime, Mr. Dijohn?"

"A temporary throne has been organised in Christmas Decorations," said Russell loftily. He made for the door, then paused and turned back. "You're amused, Mr. Toby, I can see that," he said rapidly. "You think all this is trivial, I suppose. But it means a lot to a lot of children, you know. And Ben would have been the first to want us to move heaven and earth to avoid disappointing a single child."

"Of course." Toby bowed his head over his notebook and Russell turned on his heel and left the room. Two seconds elapsed.

"Mr. Dijohn!" Toby bellowed, without raising his head, and waited. The young man's startled face reappeared in the doorway. "Sorry, Mr. Dijohn," murmured Toby. "Just one more thing. Our funny little friend yesterday. Did she meet Santa at all?"

"Our funny little . . . Verity Birdwood, you mean?" squeaked Russell. "Yes, well, yes, she did. Of course she did. Why?"

"Just wondering." Toby tapped his notebook and looked up at him, smiling. "Send Santa's helper in as you go, will you?"

The young man nodded wordlessly, and made his escape.

Toby swivelled his chair so as to turn his smile on Milson, upright in his corner. "All right there, mate?" he leered. "Keep your wits about you now."

Milson's stony expression remained unchanged. Toby's smile broadened.

· · ·

"So Mr. Dijohn asked you to stand at the door of the changing room and stop anyone going in, and not to look in yourself, is that right, Miss Stack?"

Esme nodded, compressing her pale lips. Her whole face was very pale, Toby thought, and his eyes dropped to the thin fingers that twisted convulsively together on the girl's lap. She drew a quick breath. The hands tightened and stilled.

"Why didn't you do what he said, then?" asked Toby mildly.

"I was curious," she said dully. "And then, once I had looked in, I . . . lost my head, I suppose, and then seeing Ernie Simpson suddenly appear gave me another fright and then he just walked past me and tripped over the carton Russell Dijohn left, and . . ."

"Yes, I can see how it happened." Toby paused. "Pity, of course. Bit of a mess there now, isn't there? Not, you might say, an untouched murder scene."

She shuddered. "Poor Ernie. It was so horrible. He got it all over him. The blood." She shuddered again. "There was so much of it. He was rolling in it. His coat, and face and hands and . . . everywhere. He . . ." Her voice began to tremble and her hands to twist again, uncontrollably.

"Don't get upset now, Esme. Be a good little Santa's helper." Toby patted her shaking arm. "You can go in a minute. Just tell me one last thing. Did Ben Bluff seem to you to be worried or upset or different in any way yesterday? Take your time."

"He was upset about something, but I don't know what," the girl whispered. "He said he hadn't slept well the night before. He said he had a bad headache. He took some pills and lay down, and . . ." Her voice trailed off and her eyes widened slightly. Toby pounced.

"Who gave him the pills, Esme?"

"Oh . . . um . . . oh, I don't remember. I don't know," she gasped. "He probably had some of his own, don't you think?"

"Maybe." Toby tapped his tiny notebook, smiling at her. "And when exactly did he take these pills?"

"In the morning. At his tea break."

"And the headache went away?"

She nodded vigorously. "Oh, yes. He said he felt much better. He gave an interview to the ABC lady at lunchtime, and he was fine all afternoon. Grumpy, but no headache."

"You last saw him when?"

"At five-thirty, about. He was having a cup of tea in his changing room. He always did that after work. I can't get out of the place fast enough myself but he always hung around for a while, like a head of department, though there was no earthly need for it. I change in the staff toilet, but Russell Dijohn insists I leave my costume with Ben's stuff overnight, for safety, though who'd want it I can't imagine. Anyway, last night I hung it up on the rack as usual and said good-bye to him. Then I went out and said good-bye to the others, and went down to join my mother. We went home together. She'll tell you." She looked at him defiantly.

"No problem, Esme. Now tell me, what was Ben Bluff wearing when you saw him drinking his tea?"

She stared at him. "He was wearing his Santa costume, of course."

"Beard and all?" Toby held his breath.

Esme Stack smiled, for the first time since the interview began. "Oh, no. You can't wear a beard like that and drink a mug of tea!"

"Ah, yes, silly of me." Toby kept a poker face. Well, he deserved to be disappointed. It was a mad sort of hare to have started chasing. He prickled with irritation at the thought of Milson's amusement.

"When you say you said good-bye to the others, what others do you mean exactly?" he asked, more curtly than he'd meant.

She flinched. "If it really matters, Mr. Silvester and Ernie Simpson, who were doing the money, and Annie Lee, one of the girls. They'll tell you. They all said good-bye and saw me go to the escalator! Look, can I go now?" Her voice was rising, and her fingers had started to twist again. Toby sighed.

"All right, Miss Stack, thank you for your help."

She threw back her head, stood up and left the room, her hands firmly clasped in front of her. She didn't look back.

"What do you think, Milson?" asked Toby, without moving.

"She's keeping something back," said Milson in his thin voice. "She's nervy. She doesn't like her job. She didn't much like Ben Bluff, but she does like Ernie Simpson. And"—his voice took on a slightly different tone—"it was definitely Ben Bluff she saw drinking tea in the changing room at five-thirty."

Toby spun round to look narrowly at his assistant. Milson stared back, and only a slight twitch at the corner of his mouth betrayed him.

"Call Verity Birdwood, will you, Milson? Tell her to get over here at, say, eleven-thirty," Toby said casually. "I'd like to hear what she has to say." That'll wipe the smile off your face, you smart bastard, he thought viciously. And he was right.

"So who do you think did it? You tell me, then I'll tell you." Birdie leaned forward over the desk, thin, freckled hands clasped, amber eyes sparkling behind the thick glasses.

Toby shook his head at her. "You love this, don't you?" he said ruefully. He'd called her in partly to spite Milson and partly because it was true that she might help. God knows, she had in the past. But her undisguised relish at the prospect of a murder enquiry sometimes unnerved him. Funny-looking little mouse that she was, she was as cold-hearted as a snake when it came to this sort of situation.

She shrugged, and the light died out of her eyes; leaving them opaque and watchful. "Do you want to talk to me or not?" she asked coolly. "I can help, you know. After all, I've already investigated this murder. I was here all day yesterday."

Toby groaned. "You were out of the place before it happened, Birdwood. Claiming magic powers now, are you? You're saying you knew there was going to be a murder, right?"

She hesitated. "It doesn't surprise me, put it that way. The victim surprised me a bit at first, but of course that was stupid. He was the only possible one to die, given the circumstances. But just exactly why it happened at the time it did, the precipitating factor, I can't quite—"

He snorted. "Oh, come off it, Birdie."

"No, really." Birdie looked at him earnestly. "You do three things for me, so I can dispose of my last little worry, and I'll tell you who killed Ben Bluff."

Dan Toby sighed heavily. "You're mad. What three things?"

"One, show me where he died. Two, let me see Milson's report on his conversation with Bluff's daughter. It's bound to be boring but surely even Milson won't have missed the obvious questions. Three, just to be on the safe side, give me the gist of your interviews with Esme Stack, Russell Dijohn, the staff of Toys, and the clique of 'old guard' department heads, who've been with Fredericks' for more than, say, ten years. Agreed?"

"I'm supposed to be questioning you, Birdie," said Toby, and was horrified at the plaintive tone in his voice. The woman was driving him demented, changing his personality. He cleared his throat noisily. "Given the setup of this place, and the number of people with access to the toy floor, and the fact that the scissors used to stab him were the pair usually kept in the dressing room where he was found, and the fact that we can't put a finger on anyone with a motive for killing the poor old bloke, I don't for the life of me see how you can be sure of anything, frankly, let alone fixing on one particular suspect. We're knee-deep in suspects, that's the trouble. You just don't realise—"

"Oh, I do, Dan, I do. It was obviously an impulsive crime, and that makes it more difficult. But we can narrow it down, can't we? Because as for motive—well, with respect, you're dead wrong about that. Lots of people had a motive for killing Ben Bluff."

"What?"

"Absolutely. Now, he died last night, early last night. Say between six-thirty and seven. Right?"

"How do you know it wasn't this morning?"

"Couldn't have been," said Birdie positively, and didn't even wait for his confirming nod. "Okay. From my visit to this place yesterday, I'd say the most likely people to feature on your hit list should be—now let me get them all—first, Bluff's boss, Russell Dijohn. He would have discovered the body, I presume, because he always came down to have a chat and deliver Santa sack goodies first thing. Bluff was being a prima donna in whiskers lately, and Russell was trying to keep him sweet. The strain was obviously telling.

"Then there's Silvester, the Toy Department head who's been with the store for years and hated Bluff's grotto gobbling up his floor space and seemed to me to have become quite irrational on the subject. Ernie Simpson, the Toys floorwalker, is another longtime employee who used to play the Fredericks' Santa himself in the good old days and was incredibly jealous of old Ben and irritated by his airs and graces—"

"And who ended up covered in Bluff's blood this morning when he tripped over in the changing room," Toby put in drily.

"Ah." Birdie raised her eyebrows, but her bland face gave away nothing. "Now, where was I? Oh, yes. Esme Stack, the Santa's helper, is apparently recovering from a breakdown of some sort, but she seemed to me to be rapidly losing her marbles again in Santa's jolly company. Then maybe, there's her mother Una, or one of the other 'old guard' department heads who could have decided to get at little Dijohn, their bête noire, through his pet—the centrepiece, as Russell winsomely described Ben Bluff, of the whole Christmas shebang. I think that's the lot."

Toby stared at her in silence for a full minute. She stared back owlishly. Finally he leaned forward. "Birdwood, are you making all this up or something?" he hissed at her furiously. "How do you know they all felt like that about Bluff? In their statements they all claimed they loved him like a brother!"

"Well, they would, wouldn't they? But yesterday they weren't so much on their guard, and their feelings were quite obvious."

"Obvious to you, maybe."

"Believe me, Dan. We've got motive coming out our ears."

"A bit less of the 'we,' thanks. I'm still just tolerating you. Well, that's just great. So now it's open slather on motive as well as opportunity. Which was what I was saying before. No one admits to seeing the old bloke after five-thirty when the Stack girl says she said good night to him. Maybe she said good night to him with a pair of scissors. But anyone could've sneaked into that dressing room. Dijohn and all the department heads had the run of the place after closing. They all work latish at this time of year. Or maybe, smart lady, some customer who hates Santa Claus just hid in the magic forest and went in and did the old man in. Someone we know nothing about. Some mum, maybe, who thought he promised her kid something too expensive, or a Scrooge type who pushed the scissors in screaming, 'Bah, humbug,' or—what are you laughing at? Cut it out, will you?"

"Dan, you're getting overexcited," said Birdie kindly. "Now, how about showing me the dressing room? Then we'll have a cup of coffee while I read Milson's report. Okay?"

"I suppose so," grumbled Dan Toby. God knew what was

going on in Birdie's devious mind, but it was pointless trying to get anything out of her till she was good and ready to talk. He knew that from experience, and was determined to deny her the satisfaction of frustrating him. But he may as well play along with her. He could do with a coffee anyway, he reasoned. And a finger bun or something, come to that. Milson could get on with the routine. Considerably cheered by these thoughts, he led the way to the scene of Ben Bluff's murder.

"She's obviously very upset," Birdie said, putting down Milson's record of interview with Jane Boynton, Ben Bluff's daughter. "Even Milson's deathless prose can't disguise that."

"You didn't think his daughter did it, surely?" mumbled Toby through a mouthful of finger bun.

Birdie ignored him. "He was seventy. Been a widower for ten years. Retired from his job on the railways just after his wife died. Been doing the Santa job every Christmas for five years, for fun and to make a bit of extra money. In between he played golf and bowls, grew orchids and vegetables, had the odd flutter on the races on Saturdays and saw his grandchildren on Sundays. His grandchildren adored him. He was very indulgent and generous, and always brought them wonderful presents for Christmas and birthdays, but this wasn't the reason they loved him. All children adored him. He had a way with them. They trusted him. One of her boys had been in trouble at school for stealing. He'd been led on by another boy, apparently. His grandfather had been able to get him to open up and talk about it in a way his parents couldn't."

"So?"

"Just getting the picture. He'd seemed a bit thoughtful and depressed lately. Had talked to her, only the day before he was killed, about getting old and dying. Went on about how much it meant to him, that she and the kids loved him. This was very uncharacteristic of him. He didn't say much about things like that, as a rule. Said he was thinking of giving up the Santa job after this Christmas. When she asked him why, he tried to brush it off. He mumbled something about having trouble with some of the other people in the store, one in particular, and this got on his nerves. He just wanted a finish to it. He said he wasn't sleeping, and she had thought he looked tired. She tried to comfort him, but didn't think she got very far. She felt guilty, now, of course. If she'd pressed him, maybe he'd have said what was on his mind, named the person who was upsetting him. That mightn't have saved him, but at least we would have known straightaway who did it. Well." Birdie pushed the notes back across the table.

"Wasn't really worth your while, was it?" Toby raised his voice slightly to compete with "Hark! the Herald Angels Sing" being piped enthusiastically through the cafeteria. "She couldn't even tell us if the person he was talking about was a man or a woman. All very vague."

"Oh, I don't know. He was a more interesting old character than you'd think, wasn't he?"

"Was he? Pretty typical, I would have thought."

Birdie laughed and reached for the second bundle of papers without further comment. Toby watched with a mixture of annoyance and amusement as she adjusted her glasses and threw herself into the records of interview with the store department heads with the same relish as he'd attacked his finger bun. She wouldn't find anything in there, either, silly little sod. But she wouldn't take his word for it. Wouldn't rest until she'd ploughed through the lot herself. No wonder Milson hated her so much. She was as self-opinionated as he was.

He was on his second cup of coffee, and mesmerized by carols to the point of simultaneously humming along to "Joy to the World" and deciding to buy a decent bottle of whisky for his brother this year instead of the usual muck, when Birdie stretched and looked up.

"So many wise monkeys all in one place. None of them saw, heard, said, or even thought anything even faintly unpleasant, let alone evil."

"Told you."

"None of them disliked Ben Bluff or had any axe to grind with him. None of them had any axe to grind whatsoever, with anyone. None of them was anywhere near him at the time we think he died. Mrs. Stack went straight down in the lift from her department on the fourth floor to the staff exit where she met her daughter at about five forty-five. They went as far as the station together, then separated. She went straight home to tea and telly. Her daughter went to yoga class. Milson says she was extremely calm during her interview. Her daughter, on the other hand, seemed nervy and gave the impression she was concealing something." Birdie paused. "That's interesting."

"Yes, it is. I'm keeping an eye on the little Santa's helper." Toby stirred his coffee deliberately, and watched Birdie under his eyebrows.

She thought for a moment, then went on, "Mr. Popescue left the Bedding Department on the seventh floor at six, took the lift downstairs, had a drink for an hour, then met his wife for dinner. Mr. Simms of Jewellery on nine had been intending to work late and had told security he was going to, but in the end got fed up and left at six-fifteen. Both of them appeared to be shocked by what had happened, but were otherwise straightforward in giving their evidence. Mr. Brown of Books and Stationery on the lower ground floor, where Christmas Decorations also lurk at this time of year, nicked off early at four-thirty to see a movie that started at five.

"Ernie Simpson, the floorwalker who later made a mess of your evidence at the scene of the crime, left Toys on the fifth floor accompanied by Annie Lee, one of the assistants, at about ten to six. They remember saying good-bye to Esme Stack as she left the floor about five minutes before they did. They didn't see Ben Bluff at all. Hadn't seen him since he went off duty at five o'clock and went into his changing room. They took the escalator and separated at the staff exit. According to Milson, Simpson seemed nervous and evasive, particularly when questioned about Ben Bluff's mood and health during the day. He admitted to having given Bluff some of his own pills at morning tea time, to fix the old man's headache. He showed the half-empty pack to Milson—a strong prescription drug for migraine, but nothing sinister. Esme Stack was present at the time. I wonder why she claimed she didn't know whose pills they were when she was interviewed?"

"As Bluff wasn't poisoned, the pills are irrelevant anyway," Toby pointed out. "Except, presumably, that the fact that they were his made Simpson nervous talking to us. Or more nervous than he was already."

"But why would Simpson give Bluff those pills?" Birdie asked. "I can't see the point."

"The old bloke had a bad head, Birdie. There's such a thing as sympathy, for God's sake, no matter how you feel about someone."

Birdie shrugged. "Maybe. Anyway, to finish the old guard off, Silvester, the head of Toys, didn't know about the pills, or the headache, or anything else. He didn't speak to Ben Bluff all day, and didn't see him after five o'clock either. He had assumed Ben had gone like everyone else by the time he himself left the department at five past six. Obviously, though, Ben Bluff had not left his dressing room. He could have been quietly having a second cup of tea, or he could've been dead."

Birdie leaned back and rubbed her eyes under her glasses. "So in other words, none of them has a genuine watertight alibi for the part of the evening in question. And as all of them are lying through their teeth about not resenting Ben Bluff in person, or Ben Bluff as he epitomises Christmas at Fredericks', there's no reason to suppose that they're telling the truth about their movements once they ostensibly left the store. Any one of the Toys staff could've done the old man in before they went home, knowing that the others didn't like him and wouldn't seek him out. Or they could've just pretended to leave, doubled back and just hidden till Silvester left and the department was empty, and done it then. Depending on the time, they could then have left as normal, or even hidden in the store somewhere all night, and just appeared in the morning as though they'd been home. As could anyone from any other department."

"Right. And as your eagle eye would have noted, my fine-feathered friend, Russell Dijohn doesn't even pretend to have left before the critical time. He can't, because his departure time was noted by security. He worked up in his studio, as he likes to call it, on the tenth floor, till after seven, as he does most nights. He was behind because he'd been showing you the delights of Christmas at Fredericks' all day. He'd meant to see Ben Bluff after you left, but forgot to call in to Toys on the way back to his floor, and decided to leave it till morning. He thought the old man would be a bit stiff about that, but it couldn't be helped."

"And of course by the morning, jolly old Ben was very stiff indeed."

"God, you're a callous little bint!" But Toby laughed in spite of himself. "All right, smart-arse, you've got everything I've got now. So who dunnit?"

"Oh, I've got a lot more than you've got," said Birdie coolly. "But I've got to think about it. I'll let you know."

"Don't call me, I'll call you, right?" Toby heaved himself from his chair, grinning broadly. "I thought so. Well, you have a good think, now. I'll be waiting, breathless, by the phone."

"Good." Birdie's amber eyes were snapping behind her thick glasses. "It shouldn't be too long."

"Fine. You won't take it amiss, I presume, Miss Marple, if we humble Mr. Plods get on with the routine in the meantime? Just in case, you understand, that on this one occasion your little grey cells let you down."

"You're mixing your detectives, Dan. And sarcasm doesn't become you. I'll call you in the morning."

"You're full of shit, Birdwood," jeered Dan Toby.

Birdie ignored him. "In the meantime, do what you said you'd do. Keep an eye on the Santa's helper. What's she doing now?"

"Helping out at the new throne, they tell me. Christmas Decorations, lower ground. They got an old actor in to do the ho, ho, ho-ing. So she's your pick, is she? Couldn't resist letting on, could you?"

"I'm not saying that. I'm just saying she knows more than she's telling and you should keep an eye on her. That's all."

"Thank you. It may shock you to learn that I'm not quite the idiot you seem to think, and that little Esme Stack is already under surveillance. So far, she's shown no sign of jumping a plane to South America, but you never can tell."

"Are you going to question her again? Could I be there?"

"Of course, and of course not. We'll be talking to her again in the morning. Let her simmer overnight. Whatever she's hiding, we'll get it out of her. Leave that to us. If you can cope with that." With a final grin Toby lifted a hand in farewell and lumbered from the cafeteria, weaving his way awkwardly between crowded tables, packages and small, chattering children. Birdie watched his progress irritably, and pushed the notes he had left farther across the table.

She sipped absentmindedly at her cold coffee. She had the feeling there was something she'd read or heard in the last twenty minutes that was more important than it first appeared. Some little thing—not a piece of hard evidence, as such, just an idea, a thought, that now niggled at the edge of her mind, refusing to come into the open. She closed her eyes and tried to relax, but without result. It was no good. She knew from experience that she was just going to have to wait. Eventually it would come. She turned back to the reports of interview and began again to read them through. Maybe that would help. And the other thing that would help was Toby's next talk with Esme Stack, she thought. She'd feel happier if that was going to happen now rather than tomorrow. Still, no point in fretting. Esme Stack, as Toby said, would keep.

The cafeteria was filling up. It was nearly one, and sandwiches, quiche and bagels with pretty fillings had taken the place of scones and cake as standard orders. Birdie ordered another cup of coffee and went on reading.

A large woman in mauve and a harassed-looking man encumbered by a large number of carry-bags took possession of the table beside hers. The woman was pasty-faced and sweating, and collapsed into her chair with something like a sob. "I'll never forget it, Kevin. Not as long as I live," she moaned. She felt across the table for his hand.

The man glanced nervously around. "Try to put it out of your mind, Margaret," he murmured. "A nice cup of tea and you'll feel much better." He tried ineffectively to attract the attention of a passing waitress.

"Oh, but it was such a shock! Just waiting there for the lift, Kevin. Not thinking about anything. And then for the doors to open and to see a body lying there! Oh, it was horrible!"

"I know, love."

"I'll never get over it. She was all twisted up. Did you see?"

"I was behind you, Margaret, and with you standing on your toes I couldn't."

"Well, you're lucky to have been spared it. You couldn't begin to understand how it affected me." The woman leaned across the table. "It'll be a sex pervert who's done it, you know, Kevin," she hissed in a piercing stage whisper.

"Margaret, sshhh!" The man desperately flapped a hand at a waitress and this time succeeded in ordering tea and sandwiches. He turned back to his wife. "Don't think about it, darling," he urged, his eyes flicking in Birdie's direction. Birdie hastily transferred her fascinated gaze to the tabletop.

"What else do they expect? Letting a girl run around in a little tiny skirt like that. It hardly covered her bottom! It was indecent! I thought that this morning when we went to get the tinsel. I said to you then, didn't I, Kevin? Kevin?"

"Yes, you did." Kevin leaned back in his chair. His eyes grew vacant. He had given up.

"I said then it was indecent. And now look. Some pervert has got her, and killed her. And what do you think the kiddies will think? There were some kiddies in the crowd, you know, Kevin. Kevin?"

"I know."

"They say the Santa Claus died yesterday. They say there was something funny about that, too. And now the Santa's helper killed by a sex fiend. In Fredericks'! I mean, what's the world coming to, Kevin? Kevin?"

"I don't know, Margaret." In spite of himself, the man found his eyes drifting again to the neighbouring table where the small woman in glasses had been sitting. But she was gone.

Kate's house was filled with the smell of cooking fruit cake and dying pine. Upstairs Zoe was asleep, having displayed to Birdie with much secrecy the present she had made at school for her mother (a letter rack made of paddle pop-sticks spray-painted gold) and her father (pencil holder made with paddle pop-sticks spray-painted gold) as well as, with the pride of an infant miser, her own growing stock of early loot, from the desiccated-looking midget cactus from her best friend at school to the twinkling fairy-princess tiara from the Fredericks' Santa. The house breathed contentment and expectation. It made Birdie feel lonely. She couldn't begin to explain this, and took refuge in irritability.

"You can take the apron off, now, Kate," she jeered. "You've proved you're a good little housekeeper and wonderful mother. The cake's in the oven."

"Yes. Thank heavens." Kate smiled beatifically and, Birdie thought, with excessive smugness. Her voice sharpened.

"I thought you were supposed to make Christmas cakes ages before the ludicrous event. Not at ten o'clock at night a week before. And anyway, where are the mince pies, and marzipan fruit, and the pudding?"

Kate's smile wavered, and she shrugged. "Mum makes all that," she replied briefly, pulling at the strings of her apron. "I've done the cake, anyway. Better late than never." She threw the apron carelessly over a chair and looked away. Birdie saw she'd touched a nerve, and repented.

"What've you done about Zoe and the bike?" she asked.

Kate poured them both a fresh glass of wine. "Jeremy told her that the Fredericks' Santa didn't understand how busy our roads were. We promised to take her to Centennial Park and hire bikes one day. We said the real Santa would know about the roads, and wouldn't think of bringing her a bike, but would bring her a lovely surprise instead. I think we convinced her, but she didn't like it. She was very disappointed. I could kill that Santa Claus! . . . Oh, I mean . . ."

"If someone hadn't killed him already," Birdie finished, with a grin. "Dan Toby said it might've been an enraged mum who knocked him off."

"He's a facetious old bastard," muttered Kate. "But it was enraging, Birdie, really. Think how many other kids must have been promised things they couldn't have. Still, it's awful about the Fredericks' Santa. And the Santa's helper. It's grotesque. It's as if someone's trying to kill the whole Fredericks' Christmas thing. And that's horrible, because it's really magic. The forest, and the lights, and everything." She looked at her friend curiously. "What's up?"

"Oh, nothing. Just something you said. Not important." But Birdie's eyes were shining behind the thick glasses. "Sorry, what were you saying?"

"Just what a shame it was. For Fredericks'. About the Santa, and the Santa's helper."

"Some of the people there don't seem to think so. In Ben Bluff's case, anyway."

"And you really think one of the staff did it? Killed him? And Esme Stack? That poor girl! And her mother!"

"Yes." Birdie was staring straight ahead. "Toby said he was watching the girl. Not well enough, apparently. She kept a secret lunch date with a murderer. She put a raincoat over her costume in the ladies' loo and slipped away at midday. She looked nondescript with the coat on. No one noticed where she went. No one that Toby's been able to trace, anyway. Her body was found three quarters of an hour later when a down lift opened at the fourth floor. She was lying on the floor of the lift, with her head bashed in, and stabbed in the back for good measure."

Kate shuddered. "Someone killed her higher up, and shoved her in the lift and pressed Down. How ghastly. Why do you think she went to see . . . whoever it was?"

"I don't know. Maybe we'll never know. But I think—well, she was definitely keeping something back. It could have been something that had nothing to do with the case. Or it could have been something that she thought had nothing to do with the case, but in fact had everything to do with it. I reckon it was that way, and that later, after she'd talked to Toby, she suddenly saw the connection, and decided to confront the murderer with her knowledge."

"Blackmail?"

"Could be. Or maybe just to warn, if it was someone she liked."

"Either way she made a mistake. The person killed her."

"Yes. And you know what, Kate? I think I know who it was, now."

"What? Well, for goodness' sake, who?"

Birdie shook her head. "I can't say till I'm positive, Kate. And there's no proof! Now Esme Stack's dead . . ."

"Birdie, tell! I'm not Toby. I won't say a word. I promise!"

"I don't—"

Kate leaned across the kitchen table and grabbed her friend's wrist. "Tell! Look, I was there, remember, on the actual day! Lined up with all the other soft-hearted mums, hungry for lunch, dying for a coffee. We saw you straight after! I was there when it all started! I deserve to know! Hear me? Tell, or I'll give you a Chinese burn!" She moved her other hand menacingly across the table.

Birdie shouted with laughter at this ancient threat of their schooldays, and felt the lonely feeling disappear and something warm and safe take its place. The pretty, popular, ultra-normal schoolgirl Kate had been able to do just this for her, unaccountably willing to put up both with her unlikely friend's compulsive sarcasm and rebuff, and the scorn and disapproval of more mainstream companions. And the much older Kate could do it still. She felt a rush of affection for her old friend, and looked down quickly in case it showed in her eyes.

"You were hardly there when it started, Kate," she began reasonably.

And stopped, her thoughts racing. She remembered the scene in the cafeteria. Kate eating lunch and bad-mouthing the Santa Claus, carols playing, Zoe clutching her red-and-gold-wrapped present, starry-eyed under the Christmas tree. She remembered her own visit to the Toy Department when the store first opened, what she'd thought about the lines of children and mothers, her talk with Ben Bluff in his dressing room, her encounter with Ernie Simpson in the magic forest. And she remembered the records of interview she'd read with Dan Toby. One in particular.

"What's up?" Kate was looking at her in concern. Birdie pounded a skinny fist on the table. "You were there when it started," she shouted. "That's it. That's the point! It's all there. It's been there all the time! My God, the reason, the occasion, and the proof!"

"Birdie—"

"Kate, listen! And get ready for a shock."

They were eating hot Christmas cake and had opened a second bottle of wine when Jeremy got home at midnight. By this time, Kate was chiefly concerned with how on earth she was going to break the news to Zoe.

Toby didn't say much when Birdie told him. He heard her out, with his head down and his lips pursed in a soundless whistle. He asked a few questions in a mild voice, and nodded at the answers. He inspected the evidence she offered, and put it carefully to one side. Then he stared out the window at the rain, and was silent for a full minute. When he did speak, his words surprised her.

"Poor old bugger."

Birdie stared at him. It was very unlike Dan Toby to show sympathy for a criminal. He'd had too many hard knocks, been too buffeted by life, and his job, she would have thought, for a sentimental streak to have survived. He turned and saw her looking, and his mouth set into a hard line. He reached for the phone.

"Milson," he said crisply, when he was connected. "I'm coming round. Be ready, will you? With Ernie Simpson."

"We know all about it, Mr. Simpson," Dan Toby said with uncharacteristic gentleness. "Why don't you get it off your chest? It'll make things very much easier for everyone." The grey-faced man hunched in the chair before him wrung his hands. He seemed to have aged overnight. He licked his lips. "Esme," he whispered. "Poor little Esme."

"Yes." Toby leaned forward. He sensed Milson behind him, sharpened pencil poised, willing him to go in for the kill. Perversely, he lowered his voice even further. "Ben Bluff had a headache, the morning of the day he died," he said. "And you gave him some of your own pills at his morning tea break. Right?"

The floorwalker nodded. His eyes were tightly closed.

"They're strong pills, aren't they, Mr. Simpson? You're used to them. But Ben Bluff didn't take painkillers as a rule, did he?"

"No." Simpson rubbed at his eyes. "He didn't realise how strong they were. One would have done, but he took two."

"So Mr. Bluff took the pills, and lay down to rest in his dressing room. Is that what happened?"

"Yes."

"And what then?" Toby prompted, still in that gentle voice.

Simpson shook his head. "He went to sleep," he said. "Sound asleep. I knew he would. They even put me to sleep sometimes, and I knew he'd had a bad night."

"So?" Toby prompted quietly.

"So he was dead to the world—I mean, fast asleep—when it

was time for him to go back out to the kiddies." Simpson swallowed. "And I said, to Esme, 'I'll go on in his place. I'll wear one of the spare costumes. No one will ever know, except you and me.'" He looked up, and his pale cheeks flushed with sudden colour. "I'm experienced, you know," he said eagerly, willing Toby to understand. "I used to be the Fredericks' Santa, years ago, before Bluff came and took over. I can do the job. The kiddies love me."

"I'm sure they do." Toby nodded encouragingly. "So did you in fact stand in for Ben Bluff that morning?"

Simpson's chin came up. "Yes, I did," he said loudly. "I did. From morning tea till lunch. And no one guessed. Why should they? Esme said . . . Esme said I was marvellous." His lips began to tremble. "Esme . . ."

"Don't upset yourself, Mr. Simpson. So you put the children on your knee, and let them tell you what they wanted, and had your picture taken, and gave out the presents from the sack, just like Ben Bluff did?"

"Yes. Blue presents for boys, green or red for girls, Esme said. She'd watched how Ben Bluff did it, you see. There was nothing to it. It was wonderful. Anyone who loves kiddies can be Santa Claus."

"That lets me out, Mr. Simpson." Toby smiled at this gentle pleasantry and watched the man opposite him draw strength from his warmth as Milson's glare of disapproval bored into his neck. "So you didn't have any trouble? Any at all?"

"Oh, no. Not really. One little chap wouldn't stop crying. Well, you expect that occasionally. And one young mother wanted a red present, to match her baby's little outfit for the photograph, I suppose, but I'd run out and she had to make do with a green one. She was a bit upset. And there was a pair of twins who had a fight in the grotto. And one little girl asked for her baby sister to be turned into a puppy dog. I actually had to say no to that one. And—"

"Ah, a full morning, Mr. Simpson. Well, now." Toby shifted his chair and leaned forward again. "What did Mr. Bluff have to say about your impersonating him when he finally woke up?"

"Oh." The life vanished from Simpson's face, leaving it grey and exhausted-looking again. "Well, Esme woke him up at the lunch break. He had to see that ABC journalist woman then. He felt marvellous. Looked much, much better, Esme said. So the rest had done him the world of good!" He looked at Toby defiantly.

"I'm sure it had. So?"

"So he took it for granted that we'd just closed the grotto for the time he was asleep. And Esme thought there was no point . . ."

"She very naturally thought there was no point in disabusing him."

Simpson nodded. "She said what he didn't know wouldn't hurt him. He never talked to anyone else in the department. So we left it at that. We didn't tell him. We didn't tell anybody."

"So how did Ben Bluff work it out?"

"He . . ." Ernest Simpson stopped short. A timidly cunning look appeared on his pale face. "How do you know he did?"

"I know," said Toby simply. Simpson's weak defences crumbled.

"Esme saw him rummaging in the sack and muttering, about midway through the afternoon. He must've noticed there were less presents than before. And there were no red ones, because I'd given them all away. She said he kept shaking his head and mumbling away to himself after that so she kept right away from him till it was time to go."

"Then she went to see him, didn't she?"

"He asked her then if anyone had been messing round with

his sack," Simpson said drearily. "And she said no. What else could she say?"

"She could have told the truth. Then, or when she was making her statement to us later."

"Like she said, if she had there would've been hell to pay."

"If she had, Mr. Simpson, she'd still be scampering around in her little red skirt and white boots, not lying on a slab in the morgue." Toby turned away so as not to see the man's crumpling face. "Thank you, Mr. Simpson. You can go. We'll ask you to sign a statement in due course."

With grim amusement Toby watched Milson's face freeze in disapproval as Ernie Simpson left the room. "Something wrong, Milson?" he enquired nastily.

"He was about to crack, sir. I don't understand why you let him go. He'll have a chance to recover now," said Milson, obviously retaining his deferential tone with difficulty. "It's your prerogative, of course, but I would have thought you'd want to make an arrest as quickly as possible."

"What a good idea, Milson! Make an arrest as quickly as possible. An excellent plan, yes." Toby rubbed his hands and grinned wolfishly at his companion's expression. "I think I'll follow your advice. Well done!"

"Sir—"

"Enough, Milson! I've had enough. Of murders, and Fredericks', and Christmas, and liars and cheats, and you looking as sour as month-old brandy sauce. An arrest? Your wish is my command. Go and get him!"

"Sir?"

"Go and get him, Milson. Your arrestee. The thief, the cheat, the murderer of a poor, silly old man and a muddle-headed, skinny little girl. Who else? Go and get Russell Dijohn."

. . .

"So they went and got him," Birdie said to Kate, as they walked towards the station after work that night. "Toby said he didn't hold out long. He was a nervous wreck by that time anyway, and the arrest was just the last in a long series of terrible shocks. He's not a natural killer. Just a thief who struck back when cornered, like the little rat he is. Ben Bluff threatening to blow the whistle on him shocked him into killing the first time. After that he thought he was safe. But when Esme turned up trying to blackmail him, and he had to kill her too, he just about went off his rocker. He was stealing stuff, and sending it out of the store in Ben Bluff's Christmas presents."

"My God, I wonder how long it had been going on?"

"Oh, for a few years. It started quite small. A pair of fancy sunglasses here, a camera there, the odd gold chain, that sort of thing. But as his power to move things round and organise things his own way grew, he went for bigger stakes, and Christmas shoplifters got the blame. Even split three ways the money was good. He got the lion's share. But Ben Bluff and Marie Dijohn, his sister, who did the pickups in various different outfits, with any baby she could borrow for the day, or done up as a teenager, did all right too. A nice little Christmas bonus every year. Enough for Ben, a pensioner who'd had an ordinary job on the railways to get a pool and a tennis court, and buy wonderful presents—all in aid of his grandchildren, I might say—and put a bit aside for them in trust accounts, too. As well as having a bit of fun himself, at his clubs, and the races. I think Toby feels bad about Ben Bluff."

"I feel sorry for him too. That story about his grandson stealing at school, that's what must have made him start thinking."

"Yes. He told Dijohn that he couldn't bear it if his grandchildren ever found out about him. The racket had started out as a rather racy sort of a scam, in his mind, I think. But this last year he'd begun feeling dirty, and a cheat, and thought he was betraying the kids."

They stopped at the traffic lights. The Fredericks' building reared up at them on the other side of the road. Exquisite decorations festooned the façade, and the windows glowed with light and colour.

Birdie shrugged. "He would've just put a stop to it, and that would've been that. But then fate stepped in in the unlikely shape of E. Simpson, floorwalker, ex-Santa. He understudied Ben Bluff one morning, the morning you and Zoe came to town. He did the whole Santa bit—not as well as Ben Bluff, as your sad experience can attest—and had a lovely time giving away presents to all the kiddies who came to see him. He gave away blue ones to the boys, and green and red ones to the girls, because that's what Esme said Ben Bluff did.

"But unfortunately, neither of them knew that the red packages were special. Only one little girl ever received them—Marie Dijohn, in her various incarnations. There were only a few red presents in the bag, and poor old Ernie gave all of them away before Marie ever got to him. She tried to ring her brother to tell him what had happened but he was too busy with me to take her calls. And she never visited him in person—much too risky. So it wasn't till Dijohn got back to his studio that evening that he heard, and as soon as he thought the coast would be clear he went storming down to Bluff to find out what had happened. Presumably they then had some sort of appalling argument, and Bluff threatened to spill the beans, and Dijohn stabbed him."

"And Esme Stack worked out what happened?"

"I think she put two and two together. She was in a position to see what went on in the grotto more closely than anyone else, after all. She disliked Bluff, and Dijohn, and wanted money to restart her photographic studio. She decided on a spot of blackmail and fronted Dijohn in his studio at lunchtime, when there was never anyone else on his floor. He just played along, got her to the lift, bashed her on the head with a glass ashtray, and stabbed her with the knife his secretary used to make his lunch. Then he pushed the Down button and hoped for the best."

"Awful. And all over a few cameras and watches and bits of jewellery."

"Bits of jewellery! I'll have you know that Mr. Simms from Jewellery says that tiara your daughter's been dressing up in is worth over ten thousand dollars!"

"Good heavens! She left it in the sandpit overnight, too. Oh, God, it isn't damaged, is it?" asked Kate anxiously, visions of having to compensate Fredericks' for sand-damaged diamonds rising before her eyes.

"Seems to be okay. At least they've got it back. The solitaire emerald ring, the hand-embroidered silk shawl and the two Rolex watches that also got generously pressed into sweaty little hands that morning have never surfaced. Presumably the parents of those children are as unobservant as you, Kate! Or"—Birdie thought for a minute—"more observant, perhaps. We'll never know, will we?"

They walked past Fredericks', and on down the street. "God rest ye merry, gentlemen, let nothing ye dismay!" carolled busking schoolchildren on the corner. Kate turned to her companion. "Ten thousand, eh?" she said dreamily.

"Yeah, mate. Bad luck for you I was involved, wasn't it?"

"Oh, if I'd realised, I wouldn't have kept it, Birdie! Of course not!"

"Of course not." Birdie grinned to herself. "By the way, how did you explain the disappearance of the tiara to Zoe?"

"We said the fairies must have taken it."

"Kate!"

"Well, we had to say something! She was so upset. And . . ." Kate looked vaguely guilty.

"And? What else? Go on, spit it out."

"And we said, well, that we and Santa had decided that a bike was okay after all. Only to ride in the park, mind you."

"Kate!"

"Well, Birdie, it is Christmas."

"Bah, humbug!"

They reached the station. Homebound crowds eddied around them. By the entrance, an old man dressed in a tattered Santa Claus suit was playing "Silent Night" very badly on an accordion. Birdie winced, but Kate put a coin in his hat and smiled. "Bless you, lovie," the old man said.

"Come back to our place for dinner, Birdie."

"I can't. I should work. I've still got to get that stupid story set up."

"Jeremy's making lasagne. I've got mince pies for dessert. I bought them today. And some fudge."

"With nuts on?"

"Of course. Nothing but the best."

"Well, all right. Why should I flog myself? No one else is."

"Quite right."

Birdie dug in her pocket and pulled out a crumpled note. Without looking at Kate she walked over and plumped it into the accordion man's hat. His eyes widened in surprise as the denomination registered, and he grinned a huge, gap-toothed grin at her rapidly departing back, totally forgetting his ritual blessing.

"For luck," Birdie said hastily, avoiding Kate's astonished eyes.

"Yes, but heavens—"

"Well, he obviously needs it more than I do. And honestly, Kate," said Verity Birdwood, "it *is* Christmas, after all."